For Tess, Robert, Ann,
Jonathan and David

Patrick Devaney was born in Croghan, Co Roscommon. He worked for eleven years as a draughtsman in New York City before returning to Ireland to teach. His published work includes three novels for teenagers, *Rua the Red Grouse*, *The Stranger and the Pooka* and *The Psychic Edge*, a novel for adults, *Through the Gate of Ivory*, and a collection of poems, *Searching for Updraughts*. He lives in Maynooth and until recently taught in the local post-primary school.

Acknowledgements

My thanks are due to my wife Cheryl for patiently typing the manuscript, reading the proofs and offering cogent criticism; to my children, Clare, Deirdre, Aileen and Conor and in particular Catherine, who gave invaluable insights into the mindsets and constantly changing argot of teenagers; to my sister Christina who from the earliest stages read the ms and offered helpful advice; to Matthew Hamilton for obtaining the words of Eminem songs; to my former colleagues in Maynooth Post-Primary, Michael and Rena O'Donnell, Kathleen O'Leary and Carmen Creighton for reading and evaluating the ms, Noel McWeeney for his observations, Senan Griffin and Willie Coughlan for information about County Council procedure, and to Íde Ní Uallacháin, for assisting with the Irish translations; to students Eleanor Creighton, Carmel Cushen, Clare Martin, Áine O'Neill and Fergal O'Neill for taking time to read and criticise the ms and to Ade Adeyemi and, especially, Seun Ogundele for providing me with some insight into their rich Yoruba language and culture; to Miriam Gormally and Aidan Kearney for evaluating the ms; and finally, to my excellent and patient editor, Una Whelan, whose informed criticisms obliged me time and again to revise and improve the various drafts.

Contents

'D'aithle na bhfileadh n-uasal,
truaghsan timheal an tsaoghail . . .'

'The high poets are gone
And I mourn for the world's waning . . .'

Dáibhí Ó Bruadair (c. 1625–1698)
Translated by Thomas Kinsella

'For each age is a dream that is dying,
Or one that is coming to birth.'

Arthur O'Shaughnessy, 'Ode'

Prologue

With a frown on his craggy features, Ray Kelly lowered the binoculars. He was sitting in the Land Rover with his youthful assistant, Paul O'Neill, who was devouring a prawn sandwich. They were parked under a beech tree about two hundred metres from the rear entrance to Cherryfield House. Senator Tadhg Higgins, their employer, had asked them to keep watch. On a number of occasions, soon after the workmen who were repairing the stonework had left, somebody had gained access to the house and taken food and small ornaments from the pantry and bedrooms. The housekeeper, Maisie McShane, was terrified and had threatened to quit unless something was done. However, Cherryfield House was so large it was difficult to guard effectively. Despite the security lights there were unlit corners, by walls, under shrubs and behind boxwood hedges, where an intruder could lurk and once inside there were dozens of empty rooms in which to hide.

'How can you eat that stuff?' Ray indicated the prawn sandwich. 'Those things look like baby mice.'

'They taste great.' Mark licked his lips. 'You should try them.'

'No thanks,' Ray sniffed. 'That's the trouble with your generation, you'll eat any bloody thing: Chinese, African, Thai. What's wrong with ham 'n' cheese or a plain honest-to-goodness roast beef sandwich? Eh?'

'Mad cow disease!' Mark grinned. 'Can I borrow those?'

'Just for a minute.' Ray handed him the binoculars. 'And while you're at it turn off that jungle music. You'll scare off the blasted burglars.'

'That's gangsta rap and it sure beats the diddle-e-i-di stuff you listen to.' Mark switched off the dashboard radio. 'Who do you think is doing the break-ins?'

'Search me!' Ray shrugged. 'It could be knackers or that git John Cox and his mates. It could even be one of the workmen: they know the layout of the place so it would be easy for one of them to wait round till dusk and prise up a window. Anyway, my hunch is we won't catch our man this evening; it's too soon after the last break-in.'

'Wait a sec!' Mark spoke in an excited whisper. 'Look!'

Ray scanned the house with the binoculars. 'I can't see a damn thing in this light,' he protested.

'On the scaffolding,' Mark directed. 'Half way up.'

'Where?' Ray adjusted the focus. 'Bloody hell! It's a coloured bloke! Keep an eye on him while I contact the boss.' He handed over the binoculars, then phoned Senator Higgins on his mobile.

'Boss, we've hit pay dirt! There's a Black git climbing the scaffolding . . . Oh I'd say about fourteen or fifteen. Yes, yes. I understand: you don't want me to contact the guards. All right then, we'll try to nab him when he comes out. Right . . . Right. It's probably one of them refugees . . . Right, Boss . . . I'll do that. Right.'

'What did he say?' Mark demanded.

'You heard,' Ray shook his head. 'We have to deal with him ourselves. I'll use the hurley and you'd better take the wheel brace – he may be carrying a knife.'

'I think I know who it is.' Mark kept the binoculars pressed to his eyes. 'It's that fella that's living in the hunting lodge with the hippie woman.'

'Are you sure?' Ray grabbed the binoculars only to see the blurred outline of the thief disappearing over the roof parapet. Quickly he phoned the senator again, then after a terse conversation pocketed the mobile.

'Change of plan,' he announced. 'We're to let him come out then turn on the headlights to show him he's been spotted. But that's it – no pursuit, no roughing up, no reporting him to the guards.'

'Why?' Mark asked in disbelief.

'Who knows?' Ray shrugged. 'Maybe with the plan for the new golf course under way the senator doesn't want any negative publicity. No doubt he'll deal with the matter himself in his own good time. I only hope Maisie McShane will be satisfied.'

Chapter 1

Johnno stood among Scots pines growing on the bank between the canal towpath and the road to Lisheen. Above him rooks were winging like giant bats to their roost in Cherryfield, the big demesne whose nine-foot wall rose like a prison enclosure beyond the speeding traffic. Beech trees grew behind the wall and in one spot a branch had half fallen so that it seemed like an arm reaching down to an aspiring climber.

Johnno drew deeply on the joint held between his thumb and index finger while he contemplated the branch. The shelter beside him that he, Mack and Muller had constructed during January was proving too frail to keep out the night chills, especially if there was a breeze like the one now blowing across the canal. There was an empty gamekeeper's lodge beside the lake in Cherryfield, which, according to Muller's old lad, was still in good nick. Should he check it out?

If he broke into the lodge, it would be easy to collect enough wood for a fire and he could lay his sleeping bag on the hearth. The only trouble was that if Kelly, the farm manager, caught him, he would be up again before that self-righteous bastard Judge Mooney, who would probably send him to St Pat's for another six months. Breaking and entering, he would point out with relish, was a violation of his early release. Well, feck Mooney! He could take a running jump at himself like the other fascist pigs ruling the roost in Lisheen.

Quickly Johnno drew back the old carpet that served as the front wall of the shelter and after rolling up his sleeping bag and pocketing a can of lager, set off across the road, dodging cars that already had their headlights on. The branch was not as convenient as he had judged but he eventually succeeded in pulling himself up the wall and dropped down on the far side.

While he was getting his breath back a deep honking drew his eye upward to where a great black crow was observing him from a treetop. The crow flew off and Johnno watched it sailing above the vast open field before disappearing into the wood that bordered the lake. For some indefinite reason he felt uneasy. Was somebody watching him, waiting to raise the alarm once he left the cover of the trees? The demesne was closed to the public, its two entrances guarded by massive iron gates that only opened if you pressed the right combination of buttons. Should he wait till dusk gave way to darkness before crossing the field? In for a penny; in for a pound . . .

Nonchalantly he strode into the open and, vaulting an

electric cattle fence, reached the driveway curving down past the wood. Suddenly his heart skipped a beat; the headlights of a car were approaching from the direction of Cherryfield House. There was no time to lose. Sprinting desperately he reached the edge of the wood just as the car swept past, its wheels crunching the gravel. With any luck the driver hadn't spotted him. Was it Kelly or one of the other people who lived in the demesne? Muller's old lad said that the owner, Senator Tadhg Higgins, had taken up residence in the Big House itself.

Higgins was one of the richest men in Ireland but Johnno had never set eyes on him except to see him once on television spouting on about affordable housing for ordinary people. A lot the likes of him cared for ordinary people. He was going to turn Cherryfield into a luxury golf course and build chalets that only those rotten with money could afford. If Tadhg Higgins spent even one night in the kind of shelter Johnno was obliged to live in, he would know a little more about the real world.

Bitterness gnawing at his mind, Johnno made his way carefully up the dark driveway, that in places was almost overgrown with rhododendrons. Occasionally his runners sank in muddy patches or a branch threatened to blind him. Gradually the driveway widened and he could hear the soft thunder of falling water. Above him giant evergreens sighed eerily in the breeze.

He rounded a bend and there, blocking his advance,

was the lodge, its antique chimney pots jutting up like a skeleton's fingers. At that moment a twig snapped somewhere among the trees. Despite himself Johnno felt a twinge of superstitious fear. Then he gave a start as something whizzed past his head and landed with a soft thud on the ground. He bent and located a pinecone. Anxiously he scanned the trees but it was too dark to make out details. If only he had brought the damn torch. An unusual, plucking sound reached his ears then some object glanced off his shoulder. Picking up a stone, he threw it at the spot from which he judged the missile had come. There was the flittering noise of the stone hurtling through twigs, followed by the patter of retreating footsteps, then silence.

Telling himself that his attacker had scampered, Johnno forced himself to approach the house. Faintly, below the purl and swash of tumbling water, he heard music, weird, jangling notes like the soundtrack of a sci-fi movie. Tiptoeing to a window protected with iron bars he peered through one of the diamond-shaped panes. The glass was too thick to see anything clearly but there was a faint glow inside that might be coming from a lamp or a candle. Muller's old fellow had mentioned nothing about a person living in the lodge but then it was over a month since he and the other farm workers had been laid off. Maybe Higgins had found a tenant since then or maybe he had rigged up a light-and-music system to convince burglars there was somebody at home. Johnno decided to go round to the front to investigate.

The house was built close to a weir at the end of the lake and the whoosh of falling water rose in volume as he skirted the gable. When he tried the front door he found it locked. Here too bars protected the windows, all of which were closed. Instead of the music a voice singing some foreign gibberish was audible.

Turning around, he could see the glimmer of water but there was too little light to reveal where the shore began. A strange atmosphere hovered over the place as if at any moment some dripping ghost might glide up behind him and lay an icy hand on his shoulder. Stealthily he tiptoed away, intending to check the back window again before departing.

As he was passing the other gable an eerie voice screeched '*Jade! Jade!*' When he ran forward to investigate, something – probably a cone – struck him on the forehead. Half stunned, he took to his heels and went blundering down the driveway. He didn't stop running till he had reached the electric fence and could see clearly the wavering beams from car headlights and hear the reassuring drone of their engines. When he looked back, the silhouette of the wood against the night sky had the peaceful serenity of an illustration in a storybook.

Chapter 2

Jakki sat in the candlelit kitchen of the hunting lodge listening to West African music on her CD player. It was past nine o'clock and Aidan still hadn't come home. To calm her nerves she was imagining herself back in Nirambia, strolling with Maurice outside their mud-brick house to watch the sunset paint the sky red and gold. Around them the life of the village flowed placidly: women in bright robes and head-dresses pounding millet in wooden bowls, girls plaiting their friends' hair, men sitting on the ground listening to a musician beat out rhythms on his talking drum while noisy, barefooted boys played football nearby. Well, maybe there was a downside to the scene: the mosquitoes and sand flies, the odour of goats and cows, the sticky heat – but these were a small price to pay for the great peace and serenity, the close bond between members of the community and between man and nature. Aidan's father, Gbenga, used to tell her when they were students at Trinity that 'Africa is in the blood.' Now she knew what he meant. If it weren't for Aidan she would be back in Nirambia this minute instead of sitting here on her own, waiting for her son to return.

What was keeping him anyway? Chances were he was up to his old tricks. When Aunt Margaret had written to her in Nirambia detailing his escapades, she had been torn between annoyance and guilt. Imagine: skipping school, smoking and shoplifting – and God knows what else! Poor Aunt Margaret declared she couldn't cope any longer – and who could have blamed her? What were the words she had used? 'A proper young rebel.'

Her thoughts were interrupted by an unexpected sound, as of an object flittering through branches. Could it be Aidan throwing something? Quickly she blew out the candle and raising a corner of the blind, peeped out. Her heart almost stopped: a fellow in his late teens was standing with his back to the lodge. Though it was difficult to make out details, there was something in his lithe posture and close-cropped hair that spelt danger. What on earth would she do? It was just her luck that when she needed to call the guards her phone credit was used up. Carefully she shot the bolt of the entrance door then, relighting the candle, she left it on the table beside the CD player, which was still turned on. Hardly daring to breathe, she tiptoed to the sitting room, securing the door behind her by wedging a chair under the knob.

This, she reflected while cowering in the dark, was like a sequel to last night's nightmare. She had twisted and turned for hours, certain that two giant spiders lurking in the corner were waiting to devour her. The spiders were the size of badgers, with long dark hair and red, burning eyes. Every time she dozed off they scurried under her bed and then she started up in panic, gasping for breath. If it weren't for the sound of Aidan snoring in the next room, she would have gone out of her mind.

After what seemed ages listening for the sound of footsteps or of a window being forced, she heard Aidan's voice outside shouting '*Jade*!' the Nirambian word for 'Scram!' followed by the scuffle of running feet. Without a thought for her own safety she rushed into the kitchen, unbolted the door and dashed round the house. Aidan was standing in the gravel path with a catapult dangling from his right hand and a plastic bag from his left.

'*Cad a tharla?* (What happened?)' she whispered urgently.

'A prowler,' he said in English. '*Cuir mé an ruaig air le* pine cones. (I chased him off with pine cones.)'

'*Maith an fear* (good man),' she applauded, listening until the sound of the prowler's retreat died away in the distance before leading her son indoors.

When she had bolted the door, she questioned him more fully about the prowler then, satisfied that he had just spotted him as he was returning home, she lit a paraffin lamp and turned her attention to the plastic bag. It contained half a roast chicken, boiled ham, a loaf of bread, a pot of honey and about nine muffins.

'Where did you get all these?' she demanded in Gaelic.

'From Darren Byrne's mother,' he replied in the same language. 'She said that if I didn't take them she was going to throw them out.'

'Are you quite sure?' she pressed. 'If I thought you were stealing from Mrs McShane . . . Promise me you'll never go near the Big House again.'

'Okay.' Aidan devoured a muffin. 'Now can we have our dinner? I'm famished.'

'You'd better wash your hands first. They're filthy – and so is your sweater.' She tried to hide her satisfaction at the prospect of a full meal.

'Why don't you ask Mrs McShane for a job?' Aidan enquired when he returned to the table, on which plates of food were now laid out invitingly. 'With all the men working on the house, she's bound to need help.'

'I wouldn't ask her or Senator Higgins for a crust of bread if I were starving.'

Even as she spoke Jakki wondered if she was being entirely truthful. When she had returned to Ireland from Nirambia two months ago she had moved in with Aunt Margaret, who wasn't really her aunt, just a good friend of her dead mother's. Aunt Margaret had also stood by Jakki when she was pregnant with Aidan and both of her parents had turned against her. Looking at her son in the mellow lamplight the reason for their behaviour was clear, if not forgivable: he had the short curly hair, dark eyes and rounded features of Gbenga, his father, and though his complexion was lighter, it was clearly African. Senator and Mrs Higgins had sent their daughter to Trinity to read Irish and Italian and she had disgraced them by falling in love with a medical student from Nirambia, a country, in their opinion, not far removed from savagery. Why couldn't she have stuck with her own kind like any right-thinking girl – and she with brains to burn?

Jakki had refused to listen. In the last months of her pregnancy she had moved into Gbenga's flat and he had stood by her while Adesina – or Aidan, as she later called him – was an infant. Then soon after Aidan's first birthday, Gbenga had received word from Nirambia that his father had been thrown into prison by the military authorities. He had immediately decided to fly back to his homeland but when she begged him to take her and Aidan with him he had refused. It was too dangerous. Anyone connected with his family would be regarded as an enemy of the government. Brokenhearted she had seen him off at the airport. For a year he had sent her money and letters in which he hinted that his life was in danger. Then when Aidan was two and a half years old the letters had stopped.

That was over twelve years ago. How she had survived the desertion she would never know. Her father had wanted her to give Aidan up for adoption and her mother had been unwilling to oppose him. She herself had dropped out of college and eked out a living as a reporter for *Gael Glas*, the environmental newspaper. While her parents entertained the elite of Dublin at their home in Enniskerry she had been reduced to existing in a furnished room in Phibsboro. She decided then that Adesima would be more Irish than anybody his age, renamed him Aidan and began teaching him Gaelic. When he reached four she had enrolled him in Gaelscoil Magh Mell, an all-Irish school. That was the year her father – probably because of his financial support for the government – had been appointed a senator and her mother, a thirty-fag-a-day smoker, had been diagnosed with lung cancer.

'Are you going to make tea?' Aidan broke off a drumstick from the chicken.

'*Sea, a grá* (yes, love).' She filled a kettle with water from a bucket and placed it on the range. 'Now I want you to tell me the truth. You don't really expect me to believe that Mrs Byrne gave you all this? The poor woman has trouble enough feeding her own family.'

'All right then,' he admitted, 'I got them in the Big House.'

'I knew it!' she cried. 'And after giving me your word. How could you?'

'Cool it, Mam!' he admonished. 'They have tons of food and we're dying with the hunger. We can pay them back when you get a job.'

'That's not the point.' She sat down and put her head in her hands. 'Don't you realise that you could be arrested for stealing?' And, she added to herself, this sort of behaviour will only confirm your grandfather's worst prejudices.

'I'm sorry, Mam.' He sounded genuinely contrite but it was hard to trust him. If this carry-on continued they would have to move back to Dublin and that would kill her.

It was Aunt Margaret who, about five weeks ago, had persuaded her to come to Cherryfield, a thousand-acre demesne her father had purchased while she was overseas. She wasn't sure why she had agreed to the move. Maybe it was because she felt Aunt Margaret was losing patience with her. After all, she had no job and was often depressed. No, it was because deep down she hoped her father would take pity on her now that she was tired and broken or, if he decided to throw her out, that he would at least acknowledge Aidan as his grandson.

The hunting lodge had really won her heart. It was an ornate building with an overhanging roof supported by pillars, hidden in trees near the edge of a small lake. There were four rooms: a bedroom, kitchen, sitting room-cum-study and a bathroom, and though there was no electricity, after three years in Nirambia she didn't consider that a drawback. There was a solid fuel stove in the kitchen and also a small Calor gas cooker. Old-fashioned oil lamps provided a mellow light and there was a fireplace in the bedroom and in the sitting room, where Aidan slept.

'Are you sure that no one saw you breaking into the Big House?' she enquired as she cut up the loaf.

'Somebody turned on the headlights of a car while I was climbing down the scaffold,' Aidan confessed. 'But he didn't try to chase me. Do you think it could have been the senator?'

'How should I know?' she snapped. 'It would serve you right if they threw you in jail.'

She had never told him that the senator was his grandfather. There would be too much to explain, too much to forgive. When, soon after his tenth birthday, she had taken Aidan to visit his granny in the Mater Hospital, she had immediately fallen under the spell of his exotic good looks and friendly, open manner. Everything seemed set for a family reconciliation but then, barely a year later, her mother had died. Jakki was devastated. For months she dragged herself through each day. To preserve her sanity she had persuaded Aunt Margaret to look after Aidan while she herself went to Nirambia as an aid worker.

In hindsight she knew she had been irresponsible but at the time she was convinced that she would be able to locate Aidan's father and persuade him to return with her to Ireland. The upshot was that she had spent the past three years in Africa working for the aid agency Give, during which time she had learned that Gbenga's father had been executed and Gbenga had taken his place as one of the leaders of the freedom group. He was now on the run, probably in a neighbouring country, and she had resigned herself to they fact that they would never meet again.

'I wouldn't mind going to jail,' Aidan observed. 'Jail is cool.'

'Is it?' She widened her eyes. 'You're speaking from experience?'

'No,' Aidan admitted, 'but I've spoken to lads in Dublin who were in St Pat's. They said it was okay once you knew the score.'

She was on the point of telling him about his grandfather being hanged in prison but kept silent. The only thing she had told him about his father was that he was a medical student who had had to return to his own country. Aidan had inherited his good looks and manly nature but beyond that she would not go, except to teach him a few Nirambian phrases. She had also decided to use her mother's maiden name, Hannon, as their surname: it was better that Aidan should consider himself Irish than that he should be torn between two identities. Maybe when he was older, she would tell him everything. For the time being she had more pressing concerns such as finding a job and keeping him out of trouble.

'Now that you've eaten, you can do your homework.' She began to clear the table. 'I don't want your teachers complaining. If you have any difficulties I'll help you.'

'Who needs stupid French and maths?' he grumbled.

'Stupid little men who want to pass their Junior Cert.' She rubbed his hair gently.

'Stop that!' He jerked his head away. 'I'm not a kid.'

'Then stop acting like one!' she retorted. 'You've got to mend your ways.'

'And you stop acting the concerned mother.' His voice was full of unexpected resentment. 'You should have thought of that three years ago when you ran off to Africa and left me on my own.'

'You're right: I should have.' She tried to conceal her hurt under a show of casualness. 'But we have to put all that behind us. If we both do our best, we may just win through.'

Chapter 3

Darren was in a quandary. He had overslept and arrived in school ten minutes late, receiving a caution from his tutor, Tubby. Now he had the choice of going to his locker for his maths book and arriving late in Blitzer's class or going directly to the classroom without the book. He decided to race to the locker.

Heading down the corridor, he was jostled and pushed by the older boys and a few of the girls told him to watch where he was going. Then a foot was thrust in front of him, sending him sprawling headlong. He looked up to see Clint Campbell and his sidekicks, Shem and Marko, grinning at him.

'What's up, Byrne?' Clint asked, his mohawk making him even more menacing. 'Looking for your marbles?'

'Get to your class at once!' a harsh voice bawled. It was Diggy, the vice principal.

Darren began frantically pushing books back into his school bag, some of them already trampled on.

'In trouble again, Byrne?' Diggy was unsympathetic. Darren said nothing. It was best to keep your mouth shut where teachers were concerned.

'Why are you here, instead of in Mr Neary's room?' Diggy demanded.

'I was going to my locker,' Darren muttered.

'You go to your locker first thing in the morning, not during class time,' Diggy barked. 'Now be off with you!'

As Darren trudged back down the corridor he was joined by Obhua, an African boy who had come to Lisheen in November.

'Is yours?' With a broad smile, Obhua held out a pen. 'I find it on the floor.'

Darren smiled his thanks. It was hard to feel sorry for yourself when Obhua was around. His father had been beaten to death a week before he and his mother had fled from Nirambia. Not that you could believe everything that Obhua said, especially when he maintained that he had played centre forward for Nirambia's junior soccer team. Even Darren could block some of Obhua's moves on the soccer pitch.

'You got Blitzer's stuff done he gave us?' Obhua asked.

'Yes, I finished it yesterday in Colette's French class.' Darren hated French, which he regarded as a poncy language, fit only for girls and waiters. 'The only trouble is, I left my textbook in the locker.'

'Here.' Obhua supported his bag on one raised knee while he extracted a battered *Mathematics for Junior Certificate*. 'You take. Blitzer not hassle me.'

'Thanks.' Darren accepted the book, knowing that his friend was right: Blitzer – Mr Neary – usually overlooked Obhua's misdemeanours. However, this morning was to prove an exception. No sooner had he taken his seat near to Aidan Hannon than Blitzer, in his scruffy white lab coat, came stalking down the centre passage between the desks, eye darting from student to student: 'Hurry it up, Master Campbell. We haven't got all day! Yes, Miss O'Donovan? Forgot your calculator again? Obhua, where's your textbook?'

Obhua broke into a garbled explanation in his exotic accent.

'Would you mind repeating that more slowly?' Blitzer listened to another rush of words.

'He said he left it in his locker,' Clint explained.

'Master Campbell, when I need you to interpret for me, I'll ask you.' Blitzer's voice was ominous. 'I gather you've forgotten it,' he addressed Obhua. 'All right, I'm going to give you a page to copy out during morning break.'

'But I eat at break; I no eat at home,' Obhua protested.

'Nevertheless, you'll write out the page or you'll face the consequences,' Blitzer insisted. 'And don't start sulking. Do you want me to treat you differently from other pupils?'

For answer Obhua knocked his copybook and pencil case onto the floor then sat with his arms folded across his chest.

'Pick those up at once!' Blitzer commanded. 'And the rest of you, get on with your work. This isn't a circus act for your amusement. Campbell, what are you gawking at? Yes, Master Byrne?'

'I have Obhua's book,' Darren confessed.

'Oh, you have.' Blitzer's face darkened. 'Well, you can write out the page also: page 96, examples 2 and 3.'

'Then why I do the page?' Obhua demanded.

'Because you deliberately knocked everything off your desk and you still haven't picked them up,' Blitzer pointed out. 'Master Byrne, return that book to Obhua, then look in with Miss Murray.'

'Can I look in with Aidan?' Darren pleaded. If he had a choice of sitting beside any girl, it would be Mandy O'Donovan, not Margaret Murray, the class swot.

'What? And spend the class talking!' Blitzer scoffed. 'No, you may not! How am I supposed to get you lot through your Junior Cert if you won't even bring in your books? Now if anyone had difficulty with any of the homework questions put up your hand and we'll get Master Hannon to do it on the blackboard.'

Darren seethed all during the class. The annoyance of having to sit beside a girl, especially one who spoke with a posh accent, was something Campbell wouldn't let him forget. He would be slagged off for the rest of the week. And to top it all, he had got every problem worked out correctly, including the one Aidan did on the blackboard. Blitzer was a mean bastard who needed to be taught a lesson – but how? Then fate intervened: his pen – the one Obhua had picked up in the corridor – broke and a blob of ink fell on the page of his copybook. White page, white coat! Wouldn't Clint Campbell be impressed?

When the class ended he walked behind Blitzer, who was standing facing the departing students. Quickly he flicked the pen, spraying a line of black spots down Blitzer's lab coat. Without a moment's delay he dropped the pen into the wastepaper basket, where it disappeared among balls of paper. Phew! Now let Blitzer try to figure out who was responsible.

Darren was hurrying to the science room with Aidan and Obhua when Margaret Murray caught up with them. 'You're to go back to Mr Neary immediately,' she informed him coolly.

With his heart in his mouth, Darren retraced his steps. If Blitzer sent a report home, his mother and Youssou would murder him. They might even carry out their threat to enrol him in Hollybrook College with his brother David. If that happened, he wouldn't see Aidan from one week to the next.

Chapter 4

Mick Neary pushed his trolley down the cereal aisle in Euromart, looking for a box of All Bran. He had to be on guard because Euromart were replacing his favourite brands with ones of their own which mimicked the appearance of the original. Ha! There it was. Even when he found it, he remained tense. Mandy O'Donovan's mother had already cut him dead – though she had been quick enough to ask for his help in getting the streetlight before her house fixed. That was the public for you: expecting a councillor to solve all their problems after they had voted for the other side. He had his own problems to worry him.

This morning he had awakened to the infernal thudding of a hydraulic hammer. Compu-Tel were building an extension to their factory right at the back of his garden, so it would only be a matter of time till he was squeezed out. Oh, they had offered good money for his place but he'd be damned if he'd let some multinational push him around. Then the trouble in 3D with Obhua and Byrne had played havoc with his stomach. There had been a barefaced challenge to his authority and he wasn't satisfied with the outcome.

Obhua had sat there like a Nirambian witch doctor, arms folded across his chest, refusing to pick up his copybook and pencil case and after the class he had discovered the ink stains on his white coat – luckily he had browbeaten Byrne into confessing. To top it all he had noticed that git Johnno Cox lurking outside Euromart as he parked his car. Would he find the paint scratched or the side mirror twisted off when he had finished with his shopping?

As he continued down the aisle he encountered an assistant stacking shelves with tins of rice pudding. The fellow looked as if he could be Obhua's older brother but then all African immigrants looked much the same. Not that he disapproved of them. If they were prepared to do an honest day's work like the ordinary Joe Soap that would be fine. It was the likes of Obhua that got under his skin – that imp had been given free books and a chance to gain a good education and all he did was undermine his teacher's position with his grinning insolence. You could see that the other students, especially Campbell and Byrne, enjoyed his ability to frustrate Neary. Even the stream of gibberish he came out with was probably a put-on.

Suddenly his ears picked up something that made him turn around. An attractive young woman was speaking to the assistant in what was apparently his own language. He could hear words like '*Eluni*' and '*Esha*'. The assistant's face lit up as if he had met a long lost friend and he led the young woman to another part of the aisle, remarking, '*Otutu eni.*'

Blitzer moved on lest they catch him watching them. The young woman reminded him of his own daughter, Miriam, who had gone to Australia the previous summer. They had received one postcard from Melbourne: '*Hi all, Am doing fine, Miriam,*' and after that, nothing. You'd think she could at least have asked after Ben, but no: everybody, including her brother, must be shut out because Miriam was angry with her parents.

About twenty minutes later he caught sight of the young woman standing at a checkout counter and joined the same queue. He could see from her shopping basket that she was probably single: all she had was a loaf of bread, about half a dozen potatoes, a few packets of soup, a box of rice and two tomatoes. When it came to her turn she found that the money in her purse was ninety cent short.

'Wait!' Blitzer handed the checkout girl a euro as she was putting the rice to one side. 'Please allow me.' The young woman protested but Blitzer overcame her reservations. If she wanted to repay him, she could give him her Number 1 at the next local election.

They introduced themselves and she told him that she

was living in the hunting lodge in Cherryfield.

'Then you must be Aidan Hannon's mother!' he exclaimed. 'I'm his maths teacher.'

'Is he behaving himself?' There was no indication that Jakki knew he was the class ogre.

'Oh, he's a bright boy,' he assured her, 'though a little too friendly with one of the, shall we say, less academically minded students. I'm surprised that he has such a youthful mother.'

'Appearances can be deceptive.' She smiled at the compliment. 'I was thirty-four last July.'

She accepted his invitation to share a pot of tea in the supermarket's café and in no time they were chatting just as he and Miriam used to chat when they were on good terms. He learned that she was unemployed, having recently returned from Nirambia. No, she could not speak the language fluently but she had picked up a few phrases that were great in breaking down barriers. The villagers and country people were like ordinary people everywhere, warm and generous, but the ones with power and authority were different. Nirambia had enough natural resources to make it one of the richest countries in Africa, if not the world, but most of the people were living in disease and poverty. And the country was so beautiful. It was like a wrecked paradise.

'It sounds an awful lot like this country,' Blitzer observed, 'even a lot like Lisheen. Do you know they're going to turn Cherryfield into a golf haven for the jet set?'

Jakki admitted that she had heard something to that effect but hadn't paid it much heed. The truth was she had her own problems to worry about. Gently he tried to draw her out, telling her that she reminded him of his own daughter and that he lived with his wife and son just beside Cherryfield. In fact, he had chaired a committee that had sought to persuade the government to purchase Cherryfield for the nation.

She responded warily, talking about her inability to concentrate and wondering, since he was a teacher, if he could get her a cleaning job in the Post Primary.

'I could probably get you a temporary FÁS job in the office,' he declared.

'No,' she demurred. 'I had to give up my job in Give. All I'm fit for now is cleaning floors.'

'Nonsense!' The idea of this lovely young woman cleaning up after a pack of students struck Blitzer as bizarre. She was probably suffering from the effects of isolation and semi-starvation in that old hunting lodge. 'I'll see about getting you work as a filing clerk. Leave it to me. By the way, do you ever run into Squire— I mean Senator Higgins?'

'No,' she admitted. 'My Aunt Margaret made all the arrangements – she's a friend of the senator. Now, I'll have to be off.'

'Wait,' he said. 'Let me give you the school phone number. If you like, I can drop you off on my way home. Ray Kelly, the farm manager, is a friend of mine.'

'Okay.' She gave him a shy smile.

When he reached the car he found the rear window wiper hanging down. So Johnno had struck. Well, it would only cost a few euro to replace. He found that having listened to Jakki's problems, his own didn't seem so overwhelming.

'Who is that fellow staring at us from over there?' she asked. 'He looks vaguely familiar.'

'Oh, that's one of my former pupils,' he said. 'He just did six months in St Patrick's Institution for breaking and entering and selling drugs. John Cox is his name and he's bad news.'

Chapter 5

'Don't look down, Darren!' Aidan called out. They were climbing one of the beech trees on Crane Island, the larger of two islands in Cherryfield Lake. The island was overgrown with dogwood and alders, from which the beeches rose like grey, muscular giants. That morning they had taken a boat from the boathouse at the upper end of the lake and, keeping close to the reeds, had rowed to the island undetected.

'I'm going to fall,' Darren whimpered.

'Don't be yellow!' Aidan mocked. 'In Dublin me and Liam used to climb trees that were twice this high. The trick is always to use two feet and a hand or two hands and a foot. And don't look down.'

'I'm not going any higher,' Darren declared. 'If you want to break your neck, that's fine.'

'Whatever!' Aidan continued to work his way upwards. There were herons' nests near the top and he intended to photograph them with his mother's camera, which he had smuggled out of the lodge. If he got good pictures, maybe his mother could sell them to *Gael Glas*

like she used to do before things went wrong and she dumped him on Aunt Margaret. She might even decide to write an article about the herons or about the other wildlife in the demesne: the red deer, badgers and foxes. There was also a raven and some peregrine falcons, not to mention all the ducks and waterfowl. The place was better than any nature reserve.

As he approached what appeared to be a bundle of sticks lodged in the fork of a branch, two big grey birds flapped away with harsh squawks. The branch on which he stood was now bending dangerously: if he ventured further out, it might break. Nervously he climbed up an adjacent branch, only to find that the nest was empty. The herons must still be repairing it.

By this time the air was filled with alarm cries as other herons took wing. Bracing his legs between the arms of a fork, he took a photo of them and then took a close-up of the nest, which was lined with twigs and bits of withered grass. From this elevation he was able to see the roof of the lodge and the vast field beyond the lake, where a yellow digger was at work, its clanking shovel biting into the green surface. Refocusing the camera, he took a long-range shot of the digger before clambering down to where Darren was waiting.

'What kept you?' Darren grumbled. 'I wish I hadn't let you talk me into mitching. If my old one finds out I wasn't on the field trip, she'll crucify me.'

'We can still join the others when they head here after the morning break.' Aidan sat on a branch that afforded a good view of the water. 'If Avril questions us, we can say we slept it out. Tubby won't hassle us for missing P.E. classes.'

'Fair enough,' Darren agreed. 'But won't everybody see the green on our clothes?'

'You worry too much, Byrne,' said Aidan, adjusting the camera strap. 'If anybody says anything, we'll tell them they're grass stains. Check out the bird that's after popping up beside the mallards! That's a dabchick. Look! He's diving now.'

'Yeh, I see him. And what are those big fawny-brown ducks? They look different.'

'They're probably a cross between farmyard ducks and mallards. Do you see the white duck over there? She's my favourite. I reckon she hatched from an egg that somebody put in a wild duck's nest. If she goes with a mallard drake, their young ones could turn out like the fawny ones.'

'How come you know so much about birds and wildlife?'

'I don't. Well, I suppose we always had gerbils and budgies when I was young. And Mam used to get me books on nature and take me round the lake in the Phoenix Park and Bull Island and, if she had money, the zoo. That was before she went to Africa. And then my mate Liam was into shooting and fishing. We used to drive out to Wicklow with his old man. Wow, was that cool! They had a lovely setter, Rusty, that could flush snipe and grouse – but Mam doesn't like people killing things.'

'So why does she let you have a catapult?'

'That's just for cockshots – but don't tell anybody I carry it. One day me and Liam were terminating pigeons with our catapults and this old guy came over to us. "Do ye know what the pigeon said to the boys who were firing stones at him?" he asked us. We said we didn't so he told us. Guess what it was? "What's fun to ye is death to me." '

'That's stupid!'

'No, it's not. I kinda know what he was on about.'

'You'd better not let Campbell and the others hear you talking like that. They'd make a show of you. That's why I inked Blitzer's coat – to prove I wasn't a wuss. The only trouble is Blitzer fined me thirty euro and I just have till next Monday week to pay.'

'Well, I can't help you. We've hardly enough for food. What'll you do?'

'I don't know. There's this guy, Johnno, who deals. I thought I might offer to sell some dope for him – just get in on a few deals. I could scam some eejits and in one weekend I'd be in the clear.'

'Don't be a retard! Liam tried that and he got caught

by the gardaí.'

'Well, it's that or have my old lady and her boyfriend find out. I'm in enough crap at home as it is. Anyway, there's going to be knacker drinking up the Avenue on Saturday night and Johnno is always there. Will you come with me? Say yes. I came with you today.'

'I don't know. After finding out about me breaking into the Big House, Mam is threatening to move back to Dublin. How about Saturday week? If I stay out of trouble, Mam will have settled by then – which reminds me: we'd better head back to school. It's ten-o-five!'

They descended carefully until they reached the bottom branch. Aidan made his way along it, hanging from it with his hands and feet. As he neared the outer end, the branch bent under his weight, enabling him to drop safely to the ground. After some encouragement, Darren repeated the performance. Quickly they brushed down their clothes with their hands and, making their way to the boat, clambered in, Aidan with the camera dangling from his neck.

While they were pushing out from the island, a series of deep honks came from the wood overlooking the north side of the lake.

'Listen!' Aidan held up his hand. 'That's the raven. Something must have disturbed him. Let's go!'

Each manning an oar, they rowed quietly towards the boathouse. Before they were halfway, however, a collie bounded out of the trees and ran along the shore, barking furiously.

'That's Kelly's dog,' Aidan said. 'Quick! Let's make for the reeds over there.'

Pulling like galley slaves, they drove the boat into the reeds just as Kelly appeared.

'Come back here!' he bellowed. 'Come back or by God I'll have the guards on ye.'

'What'll we do?' Darren panted.

'Keep your head down,' Aidan whispered. 'He'll have to cross the bridge behind the boathouse to get to this side. As soon as he's out of sight, we'll leg it.'

For what seemed an eternity they crouched down, then Aidan peeped over the side.

'Now!' he cried and they jumped ashore, landing in water. Ignoring their saturated runners, they hared it uphill towards the field where the digger was at work, Aidan holding the camera with one hand to stop it from bouncing.

They reached the driveway bordering the field and raced down it, then, once out of sight of the man operating the digger, they vaulted the electric fence and headed for the demesne wall. Before long the collie caught up with Darren, who was trailing behind. With teeth bared he circled his prey, waiting for an opening. Losing no time, Aidan fitted a pinecone into the leather pan of his catapult and drawing back the strong rubber strips, fired. The missile hit the collie smartly on the ribs so that he ran away yelping.

'That was a brilliant shot,' Darren exclaimed. 'You'll have to teach me to use one of those.'

'Sure,' Aidan promised, 'but only if you don't deal drugs.'

At the wall, which bordered the Lisheen–Dublin road, Aidan gave Darren a leg up and then, when Darren was straddling the top, he reached a hand down to Aidan. Before they dropped down the far side they could see Kelly shaking his fist at them from beyond the electric fence.

Chapter 6

Senator Higgins urged his bay gelding to a canter. Though the weather was brisk, he was having his usual late morning ride. It was a good way to kill two birds with one stone: have his daily exercise and keep an eye on things.

Since he had purchased the demesne from Alicia MacMorris it had been a severe drain on his pocket, yet he loved Cherryfield. Back in the eighteenth century the MacMorrises had bought up entire districts so that they could create a world of beautiful parklands and elegant vistas. Now he, Tadhg Higgins, had taken over from the belted earls and their forelock-tugging retainers. No wonder his enemies seethed. 'Squire Higgins' they called him, especially that vindictive chalk pusher-cum-councillor, Mick Neary.

If the likes of Neary had their way, Cherryfield would be turned into another national park so that the riff-raff of Lisheen could traipse through it. Some people could be very generous with other people's money. They forgot – or chose to forget – that he had spent a fortune on the upkeep of the place, re-slating the roof, tackling dry rot and now pointing the exterior stonework.

He glanced across the ha-ha at the imposing Georgian facade half hidden behind its palisade of iron scaffolding. Would Councillor Neary have asked his constituents to foot the bill for all those repairs? Would he in a pig's eye! And when the house was converted into a five-star hotel, would he thank him for providing jobs for his students? Not bloody likely!

At a high point on the bridle path he halted to survey his kingdom. Before him coloured poles being used by the engineers to lay out the golf course rose from the grass. What a stink Neary was raising over that, as if it were a crime to make changes in the demesne. What was he expected to do after BSE had wiped out his dairy herd? Bankrupt himself keeping the place intact? Wouldn't a sensible man have let the mansion fall into ruin and sold off the land to housing developers? No, he was only doing what the MacMorrises before him had done, making changes that would enhance the beauty of Cherryfield, while ensuring that it would be economically viable. He was also putting Lisheen on the map: Tiger Woods was designing a golf course in Cherryfield that would be on a par with the best in the world. In a few years they would probably be hosting the European Championship. Think of how that would boost the local economy!

As his eye travelled down the lake, past its two islands, to the lodge, his heart missed a beat. Surely that was Jakki at the door? Should he ride over? Margaret O'Hara had warned him that she had gone off the rails since returning from Nirambia, where her partner's father and her boyfriend had been murdered. That was what came of getting involved with people who were different from your own – but would she listen? Had she ever listened? He had been in two minds about letting her occupy the lodge after all the grief she had caused him and her mother, but, on the other hand, she was his only child . . . Even Joanne, before she died, had begged him to take her back. Jakki had visited her in the Mater hospital with— Pain shot across his forehead. If he kept thinking of that . . . that subject, it would bring on one of his migraines.

No, he wouldn't go near Jakki till she made the first move. If she wanted his help, she could damn well ask for it. If it weren't for all that aggravation while she was supposed to be studying for a degree he would probably be *Cathaoirleach* of the *Seanad* today instead of a mere senator. Think of the impression he could have made escorting his wife and beautiful, talented daughter to functions in Dublin! And then she had taken up with . . .

The blinding pain returned. To distract himself, he turned his horse around and urged him into a trot. Gradually, with the stimulation of movement, the pain receded.

Near the farm buildings, which were shielded from view by oak trees, he came upon Ray Kelly driving a tractor in from the sheep pasture. Ray switched off the engine.

'Our burglar was here this morning,' Ray said, 'him and a fair-haired fellow. They were out in the boat. I chased them but they cut across the Park Field. One of the brazen gits hit Ben with a stone – the poor *créatúr* ran back to me yelping. The boat is still below in the reeds. I'll ask Paul to row it back to the boathouse.'

'Tell Paul to put a padlock on the door.'

Tadhg Higgins swung his horse abruptly away. In no time he was deep in the gloom of pine trees. A raven began to croak and the breeze blew menacingly through the topmost branches. 'Our burglar!' What a nightmare! Think of something practical: the sooner he cleared this area to make room for chalets the better. At half a million each they would ease his cash flow. What was that? It had to be a fox slinking into those briars. He hadn't attended any of the recent hunts because of the trouble with . . . with the lodge situation. Between scaring poor Maisie by breaking into her kitchen and now stealing the boat— 'What in hell!' he exclaimed as a sudden outburst of chattering caused his horse to start.

No doubt flushed by the noise, a cock pheasant came sailing down the bridle path, saw him and veered crowing in through ash saplings. Presently boys and girls in navy blue uniforms appeared round a distant bend. Who had given them permission to enter the demesne? Spurring his horse, he quickly reached them. They fell back to allow him to pass, revealing Avril Brogan, an attractive young teacher from the Post Primary, and – he could hardly believe his eyes – that bastard, Neary.

'Ms Brogan, who gave those children permission to walk through here?' he demanded.

'You did, Mr Higgins.' Avril tucked her blond hair behind her ear. 'I told you on the phone I wanted to bring my Third Years to Cherryfield and you said it would be okay.'

'But I thought it was only one class.' He avoided Neary's eye. 'There must be at least fifty children here.'

'That's right.' Avril was unfazed. 'I have twenty-four from 3D, my art class, and twenty-one from 3E, my tutor class. Mr Neary kindly agreed to help me supervise them.'

'Is anything wrong, Mr Higgins?' Mick Neary enquired.

'No, everything's fine.' Tadhg was icily polite. 'See that they don't wander off the designated route, Ms Brogan. And make sure the entrance gate is closed when you leave. We don't want deer straying out onto the road.'

Touching his riding cap in a polite salute, he trotted off. The cheek of that Neary to act the concerned man-in-charge with him! If it weren't for the watching pupils, he would soon have told him what was wrong – a trouble-maker traipsing round his demesne, noting every little change so that he could use it against him at the next council meeting. And suppose he found out that Jakki was his daughter? That would really put the kibosh on everything.

As he was contemplating this appalling scenario, three boys in uniform accompanied by an older fellow in dirty jeans and a scruffy jacket emerged from the evergreens ahead. They were smoking what he suspected to be joints, though they made no attempt to hide them. One of the pupils was African, with close-cropped curly hair, one had tousled fair hair and the third was a fine sturdy fellow with a mahogany complexion and dark brown eyes. He's about his age, he realised with a start, though this fellow is probably much lighter skinned and fitter. In any case, I made it perfectly clear to Margaret O'Hara that it was only Jakki that could come here. If she wanted to bring . . . if she wanted to . . . The pain in his forehead was starting again.

'Why aren't you with the rest of the group?' Mr Higgins drew his horse to a halt.

'We were chasing a squirrel.' The fair-haired boy took another puff on his cigarette.

'That true,' the Black boy chimed in. 'He up there.' He pointed to one of the treetops.

'I didn't think your principal allowed smoking,' Mr Higgins observed, carefully avoiding eye contact with the mahogany-skinned boy. 'And are *you* attending the Post Primary?' He addressed the older fellow, who stared back insolently.

'Fine,' Mr Higgins said. 'If you prefer not to answer, I would advise you to get off my property this instant.'

The fellow eyed him up and down as if debating whether or not to physically attack him then turned on his heel and sauntered over to a path that led to the boundary wall.

'What's his name?' Mr Higgins asked the boys.

'We don't know.' The fair-haired one cast a warning glance at his companions. 'We just met him a short distance back.'

'He called Johnno, Darren,' the Black boy declared, then, observing the other boy's frown, he quickly added, 'but that not his real name.'

'Thank you,' Mr Higgins smiled approvingly. 'Now put out those fags and join your group before Ms Brogan and Mr Neary come looking for you.'

His mention of their teachers' names had the desired effect; they dropped the cigarettes, ground them into the dirt and took to their heels. Mollified by their prompt obedience, he continued with his ride. When he got back to the mansion, he would arrange to have the combination on the entrance gate changed – he didn't want any more unexpected visitors. As for that Johnno fellow – he'd have a word with Sergeant Lynch.

Chapter 7

Jakki contemplated the readdressed letter with its stamp depicting an African bird called a darter, which the postman had delivered along with another letter in a white business envelope. The personal letter was from John Morgan, an aid worker she and Maurice had known in Nirambia. It had been posted three weeks previously.

Lapano
February 22

Hi Jakki,

I have been waiting impatiently for your promised letter. How are you finding life back in wet and freezing Dublin? As you know, we are still in the dry season here with the Harmattan blowing. Night temperatures are down to 18°C. Bami has learned to speak a few more words and his sign language is progressing by leaps and bounds. He often asks after you and wants to know when you are returning to the clinic.

Not surprisingly, there has been no breakthrough in the police investigation of the murder. They are blaming rebels allied to the Freedom Party but that is to be expected. I'll keep you informed of any developments.

All the gang send their love. We miss your enthusiasm and Irish charm and – yes, I'll admit it – those fantastic dinner parties you used to throw! I miss your warm smile.

Love,
John

P.S. The Freedom Party are going nowhere because of government postponement of the promised elections. Africa can break your heart – as can an absent friend! J.

Good old John! Ever the charmer! He was one of those idealistic young Americans who took a year or two off after college to help people in the Third World. It was John who had introduced them to Bamidele, or Bami for short, the deaf mute who appointed himself their cook.

The villagers treated Bami as if he were retarded but John had quickly divined what was wrong. He had taught Jakki how to convey simple instructions to him in sign language and Bami had become indispensable, boiling cassava, pounding yams to make *Iyan,* which they ate with soup, or, on those occasions when they had guests, preparing *cheb-ou-jen*, a delicious dish made with fish, rice and vegetables. She could see him now, grinning happily as he placed a vase of scarlet bougainvillea on the table just before their guests arrived.

As her own sign language improved, she questioned Bami about life in the village, gaining insights that were denied to most Westerners. But during this time she had also grown close to John, so close that Maurice had become jealous. No matter how often she explained that she and John were just good friends, he would grow silent and moody. And then after one of their worst tiffs, she had returned from conducting a workshop on healthcare and found— No, it was best not to think of that.

The business letter was from Mr Keane, the principal of Lisheen Post Primary. Mr Neary had informed him that she was interested in joining the office staff. If she came to the school at about ten on Friday he would see what could be arranged.

Now that she seemed certain to be employed, she had mixed emotions: she would be earning money but she might be an embarrassment to Aidan. On the other hand, she would be able to keep a discreet eye on him. Yesterday morning after he left for school she had found a half-smoked joint in a matchbox hidden under his couch. Despite her own experimenting with drugs while she was at Trinity, she was horrified. If Aidan was smoking hash while he was still fourteen, what would he be doing when he was sixteen? Her first impulse was to confront him when he came home but then she decided on a wait-and-see approach – no point in having him accuse her of going through his things.

As she reread Mr Keane's letter, she was convinced that she had adopted the right strategy. From next week on she would get to know whom he hung around with. And if he complained about her working in the school she could point out that he had been the one who wanted her to find a job. He had even dropped hints that she should write again for *Gael Glas*. Maybe she would – once her mind was functioning properly. In the meantime she had Mick Neary to thank for this first step on the road back to normal life.

The thought filled her with a mixture of pain and joy such as she had experienced on receiving the letter from John. At least there were some people out there to whom she, the confused, failed journalist and aid worker, was important. She recalled her mother propped up with pillows in her hospital bed and, for a searing moment, Maurice sprawled on the blood-soaked earthen floor. Was she destined always to bring misfortune on those she loved? Even Bami had been devastated when she left him behind in Nirambia . . . How could he have understood that, in those awful days following the murder, she was too shattered to look after herself, let alone another human being?

On impulse, she went to her suitcase and took out a small ebony statue of an African woman holding a baby in her arms. It was a gift from Maurice, which always reminded her of an incident from her childhood. She was attending Mass with her parents – she must have been about three – and there was an African nun kneeling in the pew behind them. While her father and mother were praying, she climbed into the arms of the Black woman, who smiled at her and cuddled her. Naturally when her mother found her gone, she had insisted, frowning, that she return at once to her own pew.

That was a long time ago. Her mother and Maurice were dead and everything had changed. Carefully Jakki placed the statue on a shelf alongside a grotesque mask made from bark, leaf and palm. As she gazed at the ebony statue it seemed to agree. Nothing, however, not war, famine, disease or the closeness of the mask, could disturb that calm, tender countenance. For the first time since the murder she felt tears trickling down her cheeks

Chapter 8

Under a towering lime tree on Cherryfield Avenue a fire lit up the darkness. Around it eight teenagers sat on logs, smoking hash and drinking Bulmers cider. A plastic bag containing two bottles of vodka, six cans of lager and three cans of Red Bull lay on the grass nearby.

'Byrne, you're a dope,' Johnno chided in man-to-man fashion. 'I told you already you could earn thirty euro in one night working for me.'

'Why didn't you just tell Blitzer you couldn't afford to pay?' Nicola, a skinny blonde, took another swig from the cider bottle before handing it to Steffi, a dazed-looking brunette with a lip stud and eyebrow ring.

'What? And have that Nazi pig tell my parents?' Darren tried to sound tough.

'Blitzer isn't so bad,' Nicola demurred. 'He could have reported you to the head and you'd really have been in trouble.'

'He's a right bastard!' Darren pulled on his joint. 'He claimed his new white coat cost sixty euro – sixty euro for that rag! – and I could either cough up half or he'd get my old man to pay the full amount.'

'So, how much do you still owe him?' Mandy O'Donovan, the third girl present, asked.

'Twenty-four euro.' Darren wished Mandy were sitting beside him rather than between Clint Campbell and Muller. 'It's a fortnight now since I inked his coat and I'm paying three euro a week.'

'You're pathetic!' Muller shook his head. 'I'd let Blitzer rot in hell before I paid him a red cent.'

'Yeh, Muller,' his buddy, Mack, scoffed, 'You de man! You tell him, "Blitzer, you stupid old git, buy your own stupid coat".'

'Well, Byrne,' Johnno threw another log on the fire so that a shower of sparks flew up, 'are you in or not? All you have to do is sell a few Es and a few joints to your friends. Those two that were with you on the walk, the brown-skinned fellow and the blackie – what's their names again?'

'Aidan and Obhua,' Darren forced himself to answer.

'Well, they'll buy a few joints each to start with,' Johnno pointed out, 'and you can sell more in school. It's money for nothing.'

'My old man would kill me.' Darren hoped nobody could see his face reddening.

'Your old man!' Johnno echoed. 'You mean that Black guy your mother is shacking up with. Why don't you do what I did with my old bastard? Flatten him.'

Darren said nothing. Johnno knew very well that Youssou, his mother's boyfriend, could flatten the two of them with one hand tied behind his back. Youssou was built like Mike Tyson.

'The way I figure it,' Johnno continued, 'you can always flatten a big guy because you have the element of surprise on your side. It even works with a cop – straight to the Adam's apple before he suspects it. And if he does, you can always slice him.' With a jerk of his hand he opened a flick knife that gleamed wickedly in the orange glow of the fire.

'You said the shelter was freezing, Johnno,' Clint remarked, putting his arm around Mandy. 'Where will you sleep tonight?'

'I haven't decided yet,' Johnno pocketed the knife, 'maybe in the lodge. There's a fantastic looking bird staying there. She's the spitting image of Andrea Corr.'

'That's Aidan's mother,' Clint declared. 'She started in the school on Monday as a part-time clerk; her name's Jakki. Amn't I right, Byrne?'

Darren nodded reluctantly.

'And why didn't you tell me this before?' Johnno pretended to jab Clint with a burning stick.

'How was I supposed to know you fancied her?' Clint drew back in mock alarm.

'Well, you know now – all of you.' Johnno swept them with a hawk-like glance. 'Jakki and Johnno . . . Johnno and Jakki . . . ' He tossed the stick into the fire.

'How do you know she's not Higgins's girlfriend?' Nicola asked. 'He probably visits her in the lodge when Aidan's at school.'

'Don't mention that jumped-up party hack,' Johnno spat. 'The bloody snob had the gall to order me off his property – but I'll fix him good.'

'Will you flatten him?' Mack took a swig from the cider bottle that Steffi passed to him.

'No, I won't,' Johnno spoke quietly. 'I'll hit him where it hurts – in the pocket. According to the *Lisheen Leader* he's going to build two hundred chalets to go with the golf course and to do that he'll have to cut down trees, acres of trees. Now just suppose some ecowarriors were to occupy those trees, wouldn't that just put paid to the squire's plans?'

'But where would you find ecowarriors around here?' Nicola wiped the mouth of the bottle with her hand after accepting it from Mack.

'There's a crowd of them camped over in Wicklow,' Johnno informed her. 'Muller heard it yesterday on the six o'clock news. I reckon I'll drive over there tonight.'

'But you don't have a car,' Steffi pointed out.

'No prob!' Johnno grinned. 'Blitzer's Toyota will do just fine. Who's in for a bit of fun? We can hotwire it when himself and the missus are—' He froze as a twig snapped further down the avenue.

'It could be the cops,' someone whispered.

'Clint and Mandy, pretend to be taking a stroll,' Johnno ordered. 'The rest of you sing. Come on: "*My tea's gone cold I'm wondering why I . . . got out of bed at all . . .* " Louder!'

Obediently, the group launched into a raucous rendition of the Eminem hit, Darren mouthing the words. They were still singing when Clint and Mandy returned with nothing to report.

'Maybe it's the ghost,' Clint guffawed, 'the one that pelted you with fir cones.'

Johnno stared at him till he dropped his gaze. 'It's more likely to be that Aidan fellow,' he said calmly. 'Byrne, did you tell him we'd be here?'

'No, I did not!' Darren spoke hotly. 'Anyway, his mother doesn't let him out after dark.'

Later that evening Aidan hailed Darren as he was squeezing through the pedestrian exit that flanked the closed entrance gate of Cherryfield Avenue.

'Why didn't you come to the session like you promised?' Darren demanded in a groggy voice.

'Because I was keeping an eye on you,' Aidan said. 'That Johnno's dangerous. I'm sure he's the one who's been lurking outside our house. If he made any move against you, I'd have let him have it with the catapult.'

'I don't need you to protect me.' Darren's voice was sullen. 'Go on home to your mammy.'

Feeling hurt, Aidan watched his pal zigzag through the traffic of Lisheen's Main Street then walk unsteadily down the deserted footpath.

In the dead of night Mick Neary was roused from sleep by an unfamiliar noise. There it was again, a metallic, tapping sound. Slipping quietly out of bed so as not to awaken his wife, he tiptoed to the window. Looking through a slit between the curtains, he saw two figures in balaclavas forcing the door of the car.

His heart pounding painfully, Blitzer pulled on his trousers, thrust his feet into slippers, tiptoed downstairs, picked up a walking stick and rushed out the door, shouting, 'Get away from that car!' At the same time his wife began banging on the window above, shrieking at the top of her voice, 'Mick, leave them! I'll phone the police!' But she was too late. The bigger of the two thieves warded off a blow from the stick with his arm then struck her husband with what looked like a massive screwdriver.

Without a thought for her own safety Eileen Neary flew downstairs in her nightdress, screaming, 'Help! Help!' When she burst out the door the car engine was thudding into life. As it reversed erratically out the driveway, she raced over to her fallen husband, sobbing, 'Mick! Mick!' His moans were just audible above the roar of the accelerating Toyota.

Chapter 9

It was a cool spring morning, the whole world radiant with reawakening life. Aidan led Margaret Murray past a blaze of narcissi and daffodils to the wooden bridge that crossed the weir. Below them water cascaded in white foam and before them trees covered the rising ground, the beech, ash and oak still bare, a veil of light emerald on some larches, the pines and spruces rising tall and dark green.

'I didn't realise the view from your house was so beautiful,' Margaret said. 'You're lucky to be living here, not in a housing estate.'

'We lived in Dublin,' Aidan reminded her. 'Of course we used to visit the Phoenix Park and the Botanic Gardens but apart from that it was cars and concrete. Anyway, Mam reckons that when Higgins gets through with his development there won't be much of this left.'

They wandered on in silence, Aidan leading the way. Tubby had asked his English class to write an essay on 'My Changing Neighbourhood' and Margaret had decided to do hers on Cherryfield. Aidan couldn't believe his ears when she had asked to walk home with his mother and him after early Sunday Mass. Now he was in a state of nervous excitement, flattered that this bright, attractive girl had chosen to be seen with the school go-for and her son, anxious that she should not regard him as a blockhead. Darren had told him she was a swot but why should wanting to learn be a crime? After all, Darren's decision to sell drugs wasn't very smart.

They skirted the lake and paused near Crane Island where last year's reeds stuck up from the water like golden wands. Ducks were quacking, moorhens clucking, dabchicks whinnying and a robin sang his exquisite little song from the branch of an alder.

'Look at the white duck!' Margaret exclaimed. 'She must be an albino.'

'No, she's not,' Aidan said. 'She doesn't have pink eyes. I reckon she could have been born from a farm duck's egg.'

'You're very knowledgeable.' Margaret gave him an admiring glance.

'You mean for a dumb-dumb?' Aidan teased.

'Who's fishing for compliments now?' Margaret smiled and the sunlight gleamed in her grey-green eyes and pale blond hair.

'Do you see the herons over there?' Aidan asked in order to cover his confusion, and told her about the morning he had photographed the nest and how Kelly had chased him and Darren.

'What a shame he locked the boathouse.' Margaret shaded her eyes with her hand.

'Why?' Aidan said. 'Did you want to row to the island?'

'As a matter of fact, yes.' Margaret gave him an arch glance. 'I'm quite good at climbing trees, and I've never seen a heron's nest before. Do you think they have eggs in them now?'

'Probably,' Aidan said. 'They're supposed to start laying at the end of February and this is already March. Don't they look like something out of *Jurassic Park*?'

'They sure do,' she agreed. 'What's that bird circling high up?'

'Where? Oh, I see him. That's the peregrine falcon. You have great eyesight.'

'Do you think I might become a nature expert one day?' She was delighted with her achievement.

'Why not?' he conceded. 'But you would need to come here on a regular basis.'

'Oh, would I?' she asked playfully. 'Is that an invitation?'

'Yes,' he heard himself say, and they both laughed, as if some invisible barrier had been crossed.

After that they wandered along the lakeshore, watching the colourful drakes chasing each other or the occasional demure duck, while others exuberantly splashed water into the air with their wings. One drake flew after the white duck, which landed on the bank, while her suitor swung around and returned to the water.

'Will the golf course frighten them all away?' Margaret asked.

'It will certainly scare off the herons,' Aidan said. 'Imagine golf balls flying back and forth across the island – and when they build the chalets, the deer and peregrines will leave.'

'How far have they got with the golf course?'

'They have two diggers working over there in the Park Field and they've cut down some trees already. Do you see the digger nearest the lake? There was a massive oak tree growing there when we moved in. Now it's gone.'

'Aren't oak trees protected?'

'I don't know. Anyway, that wouldn't bother Squire Higgins.'

Turning away, they took a path that led into the wood, hoping to spot the red deer. As they were passing under some evergreens, a series of guttural croaks made them look up.

'That crow has a very deep voice,' Margaret observed.

'That's the raven,' Aidan said. 'He and his mate have a big nest in a pine tree on the far side of the wood: they must have been using it for years.'

'I didn't know there were ravens in this part of the country.'

'Most people don't. They usually nest on cliffs near the

coast. Me and Liam saw one in Wicklow. We tried to climb up to it but only got half way.'

'I wish I'd been there. Just thinking of it makes me shiver with excitement. Oh I am enjoying this walk – it's far more exciting than the school one. You've shown me so many things I never noticed before.'

'You saw most of them first.'

'Aidan, look! There's a wasp. That must be the first one this year. Aren't I observant?'

'You have better eyes than me.'

'No, I don't. But do you think I could be a companion like Liam – just in a small way? We could go exploring and you could borrow your mother's camera and take photos of what we discover.'

'I don't know about the camera – it's one of Mam's prize possessions. Not that she's used it in years.'

'Then I'll bring mine. It's just a cheap one but it takes good pictures.'

Placing his finger on his lips for silence, Aidan led the way down a side path. After tiptoeing for about eighty metres, they came to the edge of a clearing. Peeping through the branches of an evergreen, they saw a hind with a half-grown calf, whose reddish coat still retained some pale spots. Margaret oohed with delight. Immediately the hind raised her head, turned her liquid eyes in their direction, barked a soft warning and trotted off into the trees, followed by the calf.

'Was that fawn born this year?' Margaret whispered.

'No,' Aidan said. 'That's last year's calf. This year's one will be born in the summer.'

'You're not mad with me for scaring them away?' Margaret's expression was contrite.

For answer, Aidan laid his hand lightly on her cheek, then at her startled look, he mumbled an apology and turning on his heel, stalked off. She followed him at a distance, neither speaking a word till they arrived back at the lodge.

'Will you have something to eat?' he forced himself to ask.

'Sorry,' she did not meet his glance, 'I really have to hurry. My mother will kill me if I'm not back in time for dinner. Thanks for the guided tour.'

He watched her hurry down the driveway, looking slim and graceful in her jacket and jeans. Even her dirty runners looked stylish.

You fool! You stupid fool! he berated himself. What made you think that the most beautiful girl in the school would ever want to be more than a friend with the likes of you? She'll probably tell all the girls in the class how you came on to her and you'll look a right eejit. Why couldn't you have kept your damn hand to yourself?

When he went into the house, his mother noticed his crestfallen air.

'Is anything the matter?' she asked in Irish.

'No, nothing's the matter.' His voice was gruff.

'Why didn't Margaret stay for dinner?'

'She had to hurry home.'

'She didn't seem in a hurry earlier.'

'Look, Mam, I really don't want to discuss it.'

On the afternoon of the following day Jakki was carrying two bags of groceries through the car park in front of Euromart when she noticed Johnno, dressed in denim jacket and jeans, a woollen Eminem-style cap pulled low on his forehead, approaching from behind the bottle banks. She quickened her pace but he caught up with her.

'Do you want a hand with those?' he asked with a smirk. 'I'm just heading back your way.'

'No, thank you.' She strove to conceal her unease as he moved closer, the odour of marijuana on his breath unmistakeable. 'They're not heavy.'

'Here, let me.' Ignoring her refusal, he reached for one of the bags.

'No, thanks!' She stepped back abruptly. 'I really don't need help.'

'It's not right for a cool babe like yourself to be lugging those back to that old hunting lodge.' He gave her an admiring grin, his gaze holding hers.

Now she was really alarmed: this weirdo was telling her that he knew where she lived. Keep calm, she advised herself. Don't let him see you're frightened.

'That reminds me,' she spoke calmly, 'I forgot something,' and turning on her heel, she retreated towards the entrance, sensing Johnno's eyes drilling into her back. Once inside, she rushed to the pay phone to call a taxi. Hopefully, by the time it arrived Johnno would be gone.

Chapter 10

Tom Keating, nicknamed Tubby, the oldest teacher in the school, shuffled down the corridor through a crowd of students. From the way they were hanging about he could sense that something was up. As he pushed his way into the open he saw Clint Campbell, 'Shem' Farrelly and 'Marko' McEvoy surrounding Jakki, the new filing clerk. Beyond them Darren Byrne and Obhua were enjoying the spectacle.

'What seems to be the matter?' Tubby demanded.

'Nothing.' Clint stepped back. 'The poster fell off the wall and she expects us to pick it up.'

'I see.' Tubby assumed his mildest accent. 'The poster just happened to fall off the wall as you three were passing. Is that the truth, Miss Hannon?'

Jakki said nothing but her pallor betrayed her upset.

'All right,' Tubby remained calm, 'you gentlemen replace that at once. I see it's an anti-litter poster, a cause no doubt that is dear to your hearts. When you've finished you can pick up every last bit of rubbish in this corridor. Of course,' he added as Campbell began to protest, 'should you prefer to discuss the matter with Mr Duignan – yes, I thought not. Byrne! Obhua! Why aren't you in your classroom? Quick! Move before I give the two of you detentions.'

Jakki smiled her gratitude before leaving. Not for the first time he found himself wondering why such a bright young woman was content to be a filing clerk. Maybe Timmy Keane would consider her for secretarial work if he spoke to him. Timmy was short-staffed at the moment. Tubby had overheard her speaking to some of the African students, including Obhua, in their own language. He would have to get to know her – when he found the time . . .

As usual, Class 3D was a challenge: half the students hadn't done their homework, Campbell was acting up after his stint in the corridor and Byrne had forgotten his textbook – that boy was going off the rails. He seemed tired and listless and recently he had become chummy with Campbell. Somebody should contact his mother. He would have a word with Phil Lynch, the year head.

'Why does the boy not wish to become part of the White man's world?' Tubby repeated the question he had asked Darren. It was because of the increased enrolment of refugees that he had assigned 'Prayer of a Black Boy' for homework. The topic was risky but, on the other hand, the poem might lead to a healthy airing of views. 'Yes, Master Campbell. What do you think?'

'He prefers to be a bare-footed savage,' Clint smirked.

'Yes,' Tubby ignored the slur, 'that is essentially correct: the poet is suggesting that so-called civilised man has lost many priceless things the Black boy still possesses – and these are, Mandy?'

'Being close to nature, listening to old people telling stories by the fireside and dancing by the light of the moon,' Mandy replied.

'Excellent!' Tubby beamed. How that girl could hang around with the likes of Campbell was beyond him. 'Yes, Obhua?'

'People of my country live in villages and cities just like Ireland,' Obhua pointed out.

'Then why do they come here?' Clint demanded.

'Master Campbell!' Tubby raised a warning finger.

'They come because bad people kill us,' Obhua spoke hotly.

'And to get free room and board,' Clint scoffed.

'We no stealing cars,' Obhua flared up. 'My father die in Nirambia,' and saying this he swept the textbook off the desk with his arm then sat with a tragic expression on his face.

'We are missing the point if we think the poem has no relevance for us,' Tubby ignored the disruption. 'What do you think, Margaret?'

'I agree,' Margaret said. 'We too were conquered and made to conform to a culture that wasn't ours. Maybe we have lost what the boy in the poem is afraid of losing, the sense of magic and wonder, that rich oral tradition which our grandparents had.'

'That stuff was all right for boggers,' Marko jeered.

'I see.' Tubby made a dome with his joined fingertips. 'What do you think, Aidan?'

'I think that if we're ashamed of our own culture, we're just what the English used to say we were, ignorant Paddies.' Aidan avoided Margaret's approving glance.

'Speak for yourself, Hannon,' Marko snapped.

'*Tá go maith*,' Aidan said. '*Cad ba mhian leat a phlé*?'

'Stop showing off,' Marko retorted. 'We're not in Miss Friel's class.'

'And what is your opinion, Seamus Farrelly?' Tubby asked. 'Has the poem any relevance for us here in Ireland at the start of the twenty-first century?'

'If it means we should spend more time sitting around knacker fires in the moonlight, swapping yarns and drinking beer, I suppose it does,' Shem declared.

Waiting till the outburst of merriment had died down, Tubby announced, 'Now I want each of you to write a one-page answer to my question.' The class groaned but with the exception of Obhua – who sat with his arms folded – complied.

When the bell went, Tubby took Obhua to the Special Education room, where Avril Brogan was teaching maths to some students, one of them Iyabo, an attractive Moslem girl from Nirambia, whose braided hair was decorated with amber beads.

'*Káàsán*, Iyabo,' Obhua greeted her and she answered, '*Káàsán,* Obhua,' before continuing with her work.

Tubby led the way to a desk at the back of the room and extracted a reading sheet dealing with elephants from his briefcase but Obhua refused to look at it.

'Oh come on,' Tubby coaxed, 'you know English will be important for you here.'

'I no want English,' Obhua sulked. 'I want to go Nirambia.' After some scolding from Iyabo, however, who told him not to waste the teacher's time, he began reading, leaning back in his chair with eyes half closed, yawning occasionally.

'Are there wild elephants in Nirambia?' Tubby gazed fascinated at the tribal scars on Obhua's cheeks.

'Yes,' Obhua drawled. 'Many elephants in the bush.'

Tubby was tempted to question him about his father but decided it was better to wait till they were friends. During pauses in the reading, Obhua and Iyabo conversed in their native language, pleasant, gutteral exchanges, not unlike the chatter of two Gaelic-speaking teenagers. What had Obhua meant by that crack about stealing cars? Had it something to do with the theft of Mick Neary's Toyota, a theft that had left Mick with six stitches in his forehead?

While Obhua wrote answers to the comprehension questions, he noted the pale tips of the dark brown fingers holding the pen – was it true that all our ancestors had come from Africa? Shakespeare's Prince of Morocco probably had it right when he explained that his complexion was just 'the shadowed livery of the burnished sun'. Not that Obhua was a prince – more like a streetwise city kid. And he was bright – despite his aversion to the White man's school like the boy in the poem. On the other hand, maybe he, Tom Keating, was too much like the 'city gentlemen', somebody who had lost contact with a freer, richer world such as he had known as a barefooted boy in the West of Ireland. Had Marko intended the 'bogger' remark for him? At least Hannon had put him in his place – he'd have to encourage that kid.

When he joined his male cronies for lunch in the staff room Tubby found them discussing a planned teachers' strike.

'What do you think about it, Tom?' Phil Lynch, the union rep, challenged.

Knowing that he was expected to play the buffoon, Tubby put on a grave expression. 'It's a super idea,' he declared. 'We should close down the whole shebang and go back to the hedge schools – or better still, to Wordsworth's idea of the education of nature – you know, "One impulse from a vernal wood may teach you more than all the sages can".'

'Stop dazzling us peasants with your erudition!' Phil grinned delightedly.

'And where would you find a Wordsworthian landscape this close to Dublin?' Timmy Keane, the principal, fixed him with a quizzical eye.

'Right on our doorstep,' Tubby informed him. 'Over a thousand acres of woodland, lake and pasture teeming with flocks and wildlife. Cherryfield demesne!

Chapter 11

Johnno lay in his sleeping bag, smoking a joint. The hanging carpet kept out the east wind but the cold seeped in past the edges so that his head and shoulders were chilled. Outside the intermittent drone of cars and trucks travelling between Dublin and Lisheen formed an accompaniment to the faraway barking of a dog and the tinkling of a stream falling into the canal. Occasionally a helicopter or plane filled the night with thunder that gradually faded into the sough of the breeze. He wished he were up in a jet heading for London or New York but that required money and so far his takings from the sale of hash and E to college students hadn't been spectacular. The cops were always hassling him, and after the trouble at Blitzer's he was afraid to show his face in the village. He hadn't planned on hurting anyone but Blitzer had to act the hero. If only Clint had kept a better lookout or the car door hadn't proved so hard to open. He could still hear Blitzer moaning – just like his old man when he socked him.

The bastard had come home drunk as usual,

demanding his tea, and then proceeded to bash Johnno's mother when she asked him not to wake the younger children. The surprise on his face when Johnno told him to leave her alone was priceless, as if he couldn't understand how a son of his could say such a thing. Then he had let out a roar of rage, which changed to a strangled groan when Johnno hit him in the throat. The only trouble was that it was Johnno who had to leave the house. His mother had refused to press charges against his old man for the sake of the other children. That was the way things went: the bad guys got away with hell while guys like him—

His thoughts were interrupted by stealthy footsteps. Wriggling out of his sleeping bag, he located the switch knife in his jacket pocket. As the entrance carpet was pulled up he crouched with the open knife in his right hand but before he launched himself a voice called out softly, 'Are you there, Johnno?'

'Come in.' He switched on a torch, revealing Campbell's head and shoulders. 'What the heck do you mean calling at this hour?'

'I phoned but your mobile was off.' Clint sat on an upturned milk crate while Johnno lit an oil lamp. 'It's lucky you weren't kipping in our house – the guards called, that shithead Noel Morrison and Sheila Gately.'

'What did the pigs want?'

'They wanted to know what time I was in on Saturday

night. My old man – fair dues to him – swore I was in bed before twelve. Then they asked if I knew where you were staying. Naturally I said I was clueless. Do you think somebody could have squealed?'

'No, it was probably Blitzer that put them on to us. We should have burned his feckin car instead of leaving it at Euromart.'

While Clint rolled and lit a joint, they discussed the journey to Wicklow and the chances of the guards finding their fingerprints on Blitzer's car.

'Ah, they haven't a hope,' Clint declared. 'I wiped everything good like you told me. Did you hear from the ecowarriors?'

'Yes. Red phoned me.' Johnno inhaled deeply. 'You remember Red, the fella with the dreadlocks? He wants to move into Cherryfield right away – something about his crew going back to their 9 to 5 jobs. I told him no dice; he'll have to wait till Higgins is ready to clear the site for the chalets. The timing must be spot on.'

'You're right, Johnno. Timing is everything.'

'The diggers are still preparing the ground for the golf course so that gives us five or six weeks. Do you know what we'll do in the meantime? Start a breach in the demesne wall by removing the mortar in two vertical lines about nine feet apart and another line along the base. Then when the ecowarriors arrive, they can topple the section with poles and drive their vans in.'

'You'll have to count me out. My old man is breathing down my neck as it is.'

'No prob. I've got time to burn. Just get me a punch and hammer from the metalwork room – or, if you can't manage that, a chisel and mallet from the woodwork room. By the way, how are things going in the old nick?'

'Bloody boring – though that Aidan Hannon and Obhua are getting too smart for their own good.' Clint recounted what had taken place in Tubby's class, especially Obhua's remark about stealing cars. 'Will I get the lads to sort them out?'

'No, not yet.' Johnno thought for a while then, as if reaching a decision, he leaned closer. 'I haven't told this to anybody so if I hear so much as a word later – do you get it?' When Clint nodded, he continued: 'You know I fancied Aidan's mother – well, I offered to carry her shopping home from Euromart and she acted as if I intended to attack her. Can you credit that? What gives a bitch like that – a bloody part-time office worker – the right to look down her nose at a bloke like me? Now do you understand why I told you to hold off on the son? Those Hannons are mine: I'll deal with them in my own way, in my own time. In fact, I may just pay them a visit tonight.'

'Fair enough,' Clint agreed, 'but listen to this: Aidan is interested in that swot, Margaret Murray. Mam saw her walking home with him and Jakki after Mass on Sunday and Mandy told me he's always giving her the eye in class. But listen to this, this is just priceless. Margaret is going with Blitzer's son, Ben – he's a boarder in Hollybrook College. Mandy saw the Valentine card Ben sent her; so she's playing Aidan for a fool.'

'I'm glad to hear it but it won't alter my plans. Darren let slip – he was twisted with hash and lager at the time – that Aidan is deadly with a catapult, so it was him who fired whatever hit me on the forehead outside the lodge. Do you see now why I have a lot to settle with him and his stuck-up bitch of a mother? That's one of the things that keeps me warm when I'm lying here on my own in the freezing dark – that and the squire.'

A little earlier that evening Jakki had guided Obhua and his mother Oluwaseun, who was driving a second-hand VW Golf, from Lisheen to the lodge. She had met the pair in the front hall of the Post Primary the previous week and Obhua had introduced her to his mam, a robust woman, dressed in coat, jumper and trousers. After a brief conversation about Nirambia, Oluwaseun had accepted an invitation to dinner. If she were honest, Jakki would have to admit that she was not acting out of mere generosity; it was just possible that Oluwaseun might have heard something about Maurice's death or even about Aidan's father, Gbenga.

When they entered the lodge Aidan had a wood fire

burning in the stove and was laying the table, on which a standing oil lamp cast a festive glow.

'*E kúulé*.' Oluwaseun called out a hearty greeting.

'*E káàbò*.' Much to Jakki's delight Aidan gave the correct response.

'Why you do woman's work?' Obhua demanded, whereupon Oluwaseun slapped him across the face.

'You should help like Aidan do,' she told him.

'I'm sure he meant no harm.' Jakki looked embarrassed.

'Me and Aidan make fun,' he explained, backing away; then catching sight of the mask, he ran to the sideboard. 'Devil spirit! Can I?' Without waiting for permission, he held the mask up to his face.

Jakki smiled uneasily. Now that eyes were glittering through the eyeholes, the mask had taken on a sinister aspect.

'You put that down,' Oluwaseun ordered. 'Play with evil bring people here bad luck.'

Aidan grabbed the mask and holding it in front of his face, advanced on Obhua, who pretended to cower behind a chair.

'Put it down, Aidan.' Jakki spoke sharply. 'You heard what Oluwaseun said. After dinner, if you're interested, I'll show you how to make your own masks.'

'What's so special about this one?' Aidan objected.

That mask is a reminder,' Jakki explained. 'You know

well I brought it all the way from Lapano. Anyway, you can serve drinks while I get on with the cooking. We have Coke or 7-Up.'

At first Oluwaseun was reluctant to talk about Nirambia. Things were bad there, that was why she wanted Obhua not to waste the opportunity he now had to get a good education. His teachers said that he had plenty of ability but wasn't working. He had her heart broken.

'That Blitzer not like me,' Obhua protested. 'Tell her, Aidan.'

'He did pick on him for not having a book,' Aidan conceded, 'but then he picks on everyone – except a few of his favourites like Margaret Murray.'

'She seems a very nice girl.' Jakki carried a steaming bowl of rice to the table.

'She not nice,' Obhua declared. 'Mandy say she not be Aidan's girlfriend because he Black like me.'

'I'm Irish!' Aidan looked disconcerted.

'Of course you're Irish,' Jakki assured him. 'Now if everybody will sit in, we can start.'

'I'll just be a minute,' Aidan muttered before retreating to the sitting room. Jakki excused herself and followed him.

'Why you always cause trouble?' Oluwaseun accused.

'Aidan my friend.' Obhua looked puzzled. 'I tell him only what Mandy say.'

They listened intently to the murmur of agitated voices from the sitting room. Presently Aidan and his mother returned, both looking flustered.

'Sorry for the delay,' Jakki said. 'Aidan was looking for this picture of his father.' She placed a framed photo of Gbenga deliberately on the sideboard. 'I hope the food isn't ruined.'

During an African-style meal of boiled rice, diced chicken, soup and vegetables, which the visitors ate with great relish, they talked about Nirambia. Oluwaseun had worked in the capital as a nurse. Then evil men who hated Christians had murdered her husband. After that she had to flee for Obhua's sake.

'Not long ago in this country Christians were murdering other Christians, which is even worse.' Jakki refilled the boys' glasses with Coke before pouring more water for Oluwaseun and herself.

'The Bible say: "Have we not all one father? Hath not one God created us?" ' Oluwaseun's familiarity with scripture indicated that she might belong to an Evangelical sect and when Jakki probed gently, she readily admitted that this was the case. Her account of her earlier life, however, was more guarded. She had been born in a village in the southwest and had never heard of Lapano: 'Nirambia very big country as you know: many peoples, many languages. Better everyone speak English like here.'

When handed Gbenga's photo, she confessed that she

had not heard of him but she did know about the Freedom Fighters: 'They kill people same as soldiers do. People only want to be living in peace – that why I take Obhua to Ireland.'

'But surely the Freedom Party are fighting to make life better for everyone?' Jakki demurred.

Oluwaseun looked at her with knowing eyes. 'In Lisheen nursing home I am taking care of many old patient; that make life for them better. Men only care war and fighting; even Obhua watch war movie on television. Always men and boy love the violence – not good thing. I know.'

Jakki sensed that Oluwaseun had not been treated well by men. To judge from the scars on Obhua's cheek, she must have come from a village where tribal culture still flourished. That meant that women did most of the work and occasionally shared a husband. Yet how dull she looked in trousers and jumper compared to her Nirambian sisters in their native costumes.

'I watching *Keenan and Kell* too,' Obhua pointed out.

'Aidan not waste time watching television,' his mother retorted. 'Is true?'

'Only because we don't have a television,' Aidan muttered resentfully.

'Aren't you lucky?' Jakki bantered. 'Now, how about some fruit and—'

She did not finish the question. At that instant there

was an almighty crash. Glass splayed across the table and a rock smashed into the sideboard.

Jakki screamed hysterically, while Oluwaseun shouted at Obhua, 'This come from play with mask.'

Leaving the women to calm down, Aidan followed by Obhua rushed outside. They were just in time to glimpse in the light from the window a shadowy figure disappearing into trees on the far side of the weir.

'I saw you, Cox!' Aidan yelled, racing to the bridge. But it was too dark to give chase so he and Obhua returned to the house where Oluwaseun was hugging Jakki as if she were a frightened child and telling her, 'God save us – no protection, only God.' The table was still littered with broken glass.

Chapter 12

After a night spent tossing and turning, Aidan left for school with a headache. The rock through the window had freaked out his mother. Luckily, Oluwaseun had calmed her down but, for him, the evening had been ruined from the moment Obhua reported Margaret's remark – not that he wasn't aware that his father was Nirambian; it was just that he had never thought of himself as other than Irish. Liam and his Dublin mates had always treated him as one of themselves, so, though he knew that his complexion was dark, it hadn't been an issue. Then why were things different now? The first girl he had fallen for had shot him down because in her eyes he was Black. How in hell was he supposed to cope with that? Take medicine like Michael Jackson? Well if Margaret was put off by his colour she wasn't worth bothering about. From now on he would show her that she meant less to him than he meant to her.

Near the shopping mall he caught up with Darren Byrne, who as usual was dawdling along on his own. When he asked him to find out from Campbell if Johnno had thrown the rock, Darren refused. He wasn't a snitch.

'What's happening to you?' Aidan demanded. 'That psycho could have blinded one of us. He scared my mother out of her wits, and all you can say is you're not a snitch. You used to be my friend.'

'Leave me alone!' Darren cried. 'I've enough troubles of my own.'

'Fair enough. If that's how you want it.' Aidan quickened his pace, leaving Darren further and further behind.

His first class was history. Phil Lynch, their teacher, was showing a video of the 1798 Rebellion so he was able to slip in quietly and take his seat near the back. After that they had Irish with Maureen Friel, the one subject where he could outshine Margaret Murray – at least in oral work – but today he refused to compete. Let her do her best to catch his eye; he wouldn't give her the satisfaction of a second glance.

Miss Friel ruled the class with an iron hand, so the messers were on their best behaviour – though when her back was turned, Campbell smirked at him, which showed he knew about the rock. Obhua was with Avril Brogan for Special Ed and Darren was furtively copying his maths homework. They were studying '*Faoileán*', a poem that dealt with a seagull killed by an oil spill.

'You're very quiet today, Aidan,' Miss Friel commented when he failed to offer an opinion on the wider significance of the poem. How could she know that the image of the once-proud bird lying like a piece of rubbish on a harbour rock mirrored too closely the desolation in his own mind? Of course, Margaret was able to point out that the poem was really about man's impact on the environment. She had even brought in a letter dealing with the development of Cherryfield, which had appeared in that week's *Lisheen Leader.* Though the letter was in English Miss Friel read it to the class:

> Sir,
> The work now in progress to turn Cherryfield into a residential park-cum-playground for the jet set is a national disgrace. Once again Dublin's green belt is under attack from corrupt rezoning and the greed of developers. As an eighteenth century poet lamented about the destruction of Cill Chais:
>
> 'What will we do without timber?
> The last of the woods are down . . .'
>
> Cherryfield is an oasis in the urban sprawl engulfing every county adjacent to the capital, a lung supplying us with clean air, but sadly that lung is now under the knife. Even as I write, the parkland so lovingly created by the MacMorrises in the eighteenth century

is being turned into a golf course and the woods will soon be honeycombed with clearings to make room for luxury chalets. 'So what?' I hear my critics ask. 'Isn't it better to have an attractive golf course than a mixture of housing estates and light industry?'

Yes, I agree. But why can a demesne that is an important example of Georgian landscaping and architecture not be preserved intact for the nation? The French have preserved Versailles, the Russians the Kremlin and the Chinese the Forbidden City but here in Ireland we dismiss Cherryfield as a relic of Anglo-Irish grandeur. What nonsense! The MacMorrises were among the first Normans to adopt an Irish surname; Myler MacMorris, who lived with his wife in the Hunting Lodge, led the attack on Lisheen during the 1798 Rebellion and Lady Alicia used to walk barefooted into the village to purchase her groceries. Where was the grandeur in that?

But leaving aside social distinctions, I wish to focus on the matter of wildlife. Something that always gladdened my heart as I cycled back from Dublin was the sight of a heron

> sailing into the treetops on Crane Island.

'Miss, that's Mr Keating, isn't it?' Campbell interrupted.

'If you have any question to ask, Clint, you'll have to ask in Irish,' Maureen Friel reminded him and when Campbell declined the invitation, she continued reading:

> How long will the heronry survive a bombardment of flying golf balls? And what of the red deer that presently roam the woods and pastures? Will they be allowed to trespass on the pristine golf course or will they be quietly eliminated? Will the ravens and owls that love secluded woodlands remain when there is constant human intrusion? And what of the kingfishers that frequent the river? What indeed!

'I saw a kingfisher flying along the canal,' Marko piped up.

'*Abair é sin i nGaeilge* (Say that in Irish),' Maureen instructed.

'*Chonaic mé* kingfisher *ag* flying *os cionn an* canal,' Marko responded, much to the amusement of the class.

'*Ciúnas*! (Silence!)' Maureen commanded, then after telling Marko to have 'canal', 'flying' and 'kingfisher' written out three times in Irish for the following day, she continued:

> Centuries before the MacMorrises purchased Cherryfield the area was known as Clooneybawn, the Fair Meadow, and it is even recorded that Saint Mochua – the hermit that wrote to Colmcille about his three pets, the cock, the mouse and the fly – lived there.

'Why did he have such weird pets?' Shem asked.

'Write out that question six times in Irish for tomorrow,' Maureen said in an even voice, 'and, Mandy, can you set his mind at rest?'

'Had it something to do with keeping him awake?' Mandy answered hesitantly in Irish.

'Very good,' Maureen looked pleased. 'The cock crowed to rouse him for matins; the mouse nibbled his ear if he overslept – are we listening, Darren? – and the fly used to walk along under the line he was reading and when he paused to rest, the fly would stop to mark the spot. Now if there aren't any more interruptions, I'll finish:

> By a series of historical accidents, the peace and natural beauty that drew Mochua to Clooneybawn has survived into the twenty-

> first century but in the harsh world of the Celtic Tiger that situation is changing and we are watching another Eden being desecrated to enrich the powerful and leave the rest of us poor indeed.

'For those of you who, like Clint, are curious about the writer, the letter is signed "Diarmaid",' Maureen added, 'but as to who Diarmaid might be, your guess is as good as mine.'

Aidan figured that Clint was probably right: only somebody like Tubby could have put on such a display of learning – and he did ride a bike. Anyway, Margaret must be pleased with the stir she had caused. There she was now, gabbling away in her precise Irish with Miss Friel about Cherryfield, as if she were the one who lived there. His headache was returning.

During morning break, he tackled Mandy: had Margaret said he and Obhua were the same?

'Oh, don't listen to Obhua.' She took a bite of an apple. 'I was just winding him up. Margaret didn't say anything – but she does have a boyfriend already.'

'How do I know you're not winding me up, like you did with Obhua?' He tried to conceal his relief.

'You can think what you like.' Mandy shook her spiky bleached hair in annoyance before walking away to join her friends.

When Aidan entered the toilets he saw Campbell and his cronies holding Obhua's head down a toilet bowl while they flushed it. 'What are you doing?' he shouted, making for the cubicle.

'Look, Clint,' Marko blocked Aidan's advance, 'another black sheep for dipping!'

'Just you try it!' Aidan raised his fists as Shem and Marko came towards him.

'Leave him!' Campbell barked. 'Johnno's orders. And, Obhua, the next time you shoot your mouth off in class about me stealing cars you won't get off this lightly. *Capeesh*?'

'You nothing but a damn racist,' Obhua spluttered, wiping his face with toilet paper.

Just then a group of students, including Darren, barged through the door.

'Come on,' Campbell said. 'These two have had their warning.' And, grinning broadly, he and his sidekicks shouldered their way out.

Chapter 13

A fortnight later, just after the publication of his second Cherryfield letter, Tubby cycled as usual to school, not to teach but to join a picket line outside the front gate. As he passed a group of senior students in their navy blue uniforms, one of them, Justin Quinlan, gave him the finger. Tubby dismounted and beckoned him over.

'What was the meaning of that?' he demanded.

'Sorry, sir,' Quinlan sounded contrite. 'It must have been an inadvertent gesture.'

'I see my teaching hasn't been entirely wasted,' Tubby observed, secretly amused by his pupil's neat turn of phrase. Was Quinlan reacting to the letters – his father was a keen golfer – or to the school closure? Assuming a grim look, he remounted his bicycle. Since this series of one-day strikes had begun, the yobbos had seized their chance to get even. Only yesterday that lout Jim Mullooly had clapped him on the shoulder while he was walking down the corridor and asked, 'How's it going, Tom?' Timmy Keane had been a right fool to let him and MacDermott back into the school after their suspended sentences for breaking and entering and peddling drugs. At least their mate, Johnno Cox, had served time for the same offences.

He felt sorry for Johnno. Despite all his defiance there was good in the lad. Darren Byrne had mentioned during a class discussion on Cherryfield that Johnno was going to save it, though he refused to divulge how this would be done. He would always remember Johnno's face softening the time he had let him off with a caution after he had caught him throwing eggs at his house. With a father like he had, who could blame him for going off the rails? According to Darren, he was presently living in a makeshift hideout on the canal bank. Ah, well, if this dispute with the Department of Education wasn't settled soon they might all be sleeping rough. Not that that would bother him too much.

Since his wife had decamped twenty years ago with their two children he hadn't had much to console him, apart from getting the odd poem or article published. Now his colleagues were striking for more money – as if money could compensate for the lack of respect they were daily shown by pupils and the public. What was it Columcille had written back to Mochua when he sent him the letter lamenting the death of his three pets? 'There is no misfortune except where there is wealth.' Yes, that was it: filthy lucre . . . the root of all evil – not that teachers weren't due a raise just as much as policemen and politicians.

'Get the lead out, Keating!' Paul Duignan scolded as he reached the front entrance, where Paul, Maureen Friel and Renée Lebrun, who taught French, were carrying placards reading 'STAILC OIFIGIÚIL', official strike.

'What's the hurry?' Watched by a crowd of grinning students, Tubby donned a placard with 'FAIR PLAY FOR TEACHERS' emblazoned in white on a red background.

'If you cared as much for your profession as you do for Cherryfield, you'd have been here twenty minutes ago,' Diggy growled, only half in jest.

'Who said I cared about Cherryfield?' Feeling vaguely idiotic, Tubby began pacing with the others.

'Oh, come on, Tom,' Maureen Friel piped up. 'We all know who Diarmaid is. By the way, did Saint Mochua really live near Lisheen?'

Before Tubby could answer, an apple core struck his ear. Wheeling about, he glimpsed a head with a mohawk ducking behind the clump of bushes fronting the Science Room. Clint Campbell! The bloody gurrier! Well, that was it!

'Where the hell do you think you're going?' Diggy protested as Tom tore off his placard and mounted his bike.

'To the canal,' Tubby declared. 'I'm going to visit one of my ex-students, John Cox. We wouldn't let him back but he's miles ahead of that shower in there.'

The first thing Tubby noticed when he climbed up among the trees and bushes on the embankment was Johnno shaving before a mirror-fronted bathroom cabinet wedged in the fork of a tree. Two plastic paint cans filled with water stood nearby and further back the open front of the shelter revealed a floor made of plastic sheeting and plywood, on which a sleeping bag, various items of clothing and empty food cartons were thrown.

'Where do you think you're going?' Johnno snarled. 'Do I just walk into your house?'

'Sorry,' Tubby apologised. 'I was just cycling along the canal and noticed the carpet hanging on a pole. I didn't realise there was anyone living here.'

'Well, there is.' Johnno resumed his shaving. 'Now push off.'

'I heard you were interested in saving Cherryfield.' Tubby surveyed the newly created brown desert visible beyond the top of the demesne wall.

'Who told you that?' Johnno's voice was threatening. 'That little snitch, Darren Byrne?'

'Not really,' Tubby lied. 'I have my sources. By the way, you may have read my letters on the destruction of Cherryfield in the *Leader*?'

'Do I look as if I read newspapers?' Johnno glared at him.

'As I remember, you were quite good at English,' Tubby remained calm. 'I was really impressed by your essay on 'The Best Day of my Summer Holidays', the one where you wrote about visiting your grandparents in Kerry.'

'It was West Cork,' Johnno's voice was less hostile, 'and if I was so good at English, why did you fail me in the mock Junior Cert?'

'I think you know the answer to that question yourself.' Tubby spoke gently. 'You may recall that you hadn't studied any of the literature – but that was two years ago and what's past is past. The point now is that I would like your help in saving Cherryfield.'

'You want *me* to help *you*?' Johnno's face twisted into a bitter smile.

'Why not?' Tubby looked him directly in the eye. 'You're smart and you have time on your hands. Oh, I know you've had your brush with the law but I'm convinced that any fellow who could write so movingly about his grandparents has a good heart. What do you say?'

Johnno's expression softened. 'Do you have the *Leader*?' he said.

About an hour later, Jakki was amazed to hear a knock on the door. On opening it she found Tom Keating with an apologetic grin on his face. He had been passing

Cherrryfield, saw a truck emerging and, on impulse, cycled in before the gate swung shut.

Seated in front of the stove with a glass of wine, he told her about visiting Johnno – 'I bearded the lion in his den,' he chuckled. At first Johnno had been hostile then he had asked to see the last Cherryfield letter – had Jakki read it herself? Fortunately, he just happened to have a photocopy on him.

After Jakki had skimmed the letter, he told her that Johnno had let him in on his plan to enlist the ecowarriors in the fight to save Cherryfield. Wasn't it fantastic news?

Jakki didn't agree. After Nirambia she had felt that she would never be happy again but Cherryfield and especially the promotion from filing clerk to part-time secretary that Tom had landed for her had given her back the will to live. But since the breaking of the window she was having trouble sleeping. Now the nightmare was returning.

In answer to his queries about the window, she told him that she was convinced that Johnno was responsible. Did he know that fellow had been prowling round the lodge after dark? Only a week ago she had actually heard him trying to prise open the bathroom window. When she called out, 'Aidan!' he had fled. If Tom thought she was imagining things, she could show him the knife marks on the sash. How could she side with such a creep against Senator Higgins, who had given her this place rent-free?

Tom argued that Johnno wasn't such a bad fellow once you got to know him. He would talk to him about the prowling. As for Senator Higgins, what he was doing to Cherryfield was criminal. He then went on to tell her about his own friendship with Lady Alicia, who would turn in her grave if she could see her beloved Cherryfield now.

'You knew her well then?' Jakki was intrigued.

'Oh yes,' Tom's face grew wistful. 'You should have seen her with holes in the elbows of her cardigan and her hair falling into her cornflower-blue eyes. She told me once that when Myler MacMorris lived here he had a tunnel dug in which to store arms – of course, it was also to escape through if the lodge was surrounded. You didn't find it by any chance?'

'No,' Jakki shook her head. 'Was Lady Alicia a Republican then?'

'Not really,' Tom admitted. 'But she would have fought tooth and nail to save this demesne. In fact the two of you would have had much in common. Do you know I used to devour your articles in *Gael Glas*? Why do you think I signed my letter Diarmaid? It was a tribute to the Gráinne who wasn't afraid to take on the likes of Tadhg Higgins for bribing councillors to rezone agricultural land or multinationals for exploiting the natural wealth of Africa.'

'And what did it all achieve?' Jakki retorted. 'The

developed world is still ripping off the Africans, forcing them to grow cash crops to pay off crippling debts, selling them out-of-date medicines, letting them massacre each other because it might be risky to send in peace-keepers, buying up their hardwoods and minerals for a song.'

'Now that's the old Gráinne,' Tom enthused, 'somebody who wasn't afraid to tell it as it is.'

'Well, the old Gráinne is dead,' Jakki declared. 'When I went to Nirambia, I really believed I could change things. The country was so beautiful and the people, despite their poverty, so warm and friendly. Of course the government was corrupt – that's why I sympathised with the rebels, even though Maurice warned me not to get involved. Ah well, I never could mind my own business.'

'Maurice was killed, wasn't he?' Tom probed softly.

'I don't want to talk about it.' Pain swept Jakki's face. 'All I know now is that there are no *Tir na nÓgs,* no perfect societies. We have to make the best of what we're given.'

'That's not true!' Tom protested. 'What was it Ulysses said in that poem of Tennyson's: " 'Tis not too late to seek a newer world." If we do nothing the fat cats will gobble up everything but if we fight back, we can— '

He broke off as Aidan, followed by Obhua and Iyabo, came through the door, only to freeze when they caught sight of him.

'I thought you were going to stay in school for study.'

Jakki looked surprised.

'The woman who's supervising can't control the class,' Aidan told her.

'Hi, Aidan. *Káàsán*, Iyabo. *Káàsán*, Obhua,' Tubby greeted them then seeing the girl smile, he added, 'Have I said something wrong?'

'*Káàsán* means 'good afternoon', Iyabo explained. 'You should have said *Káàárò*, for Good morning.'

'*Káàárò*, Iyabo. *Káàárò*, Obhua,' Tubby corrected himself. 'By the way, Iyabo is a lovely name. What does it mean?'

'This name is given if the grandmother dies before the girl is born,' Iyabo explained. 'It means "The grandmother came back"'.

'Well, that's fascinating.' Tubby was secretly impressed by the girl's fluency. 'I'll have to get you to teach me more of your language.'

'You'll all have a cup of tea first.' Jakki pulled up chairs for the new arrivals before rinsing out the teapot.

Gradually the young people lost their reserve and began discussing the strike with Tubby and the fact that some students were travelling to Dublin to take part in a demonstration.

'What is the demonstration about?' Jakki asked.

'To protest the absence of teachers from the classrooms,' Aidan said. 'Margaret Murray is one of the organisers.'

'Good for them!' Tubby applauded. 'It's always gratifying to see people standing up for what they believe in. And, like it or not, education is everything in today's world.'

'I think they may be more interested in raising a ruckus than in getting an education,' Jakki commented drily. 'Isn't that true, boys?'

'Why ask me?' Aidan shrugged. 'I'm not going.'

'I not going also,' Obhua pointed out. 'Aidan show us deer.'

'Do you have deer in Nirambia?' Tubby asked.

'I don't think so,' Iyabo looked at Jakki. 'We have – what do you call them? *Koba*?'

'Antelope,' Jakki suggested as Obhua put his index fingers alongside his forehead to indicate two horns.

'That's right.' A smile lit up Iyabo's face so that Tubby was suddenly struck by how beautiful she was with her luminous dark eyes and gleaming white teeth. Surely either Aidan or Obhua fancied her. If only he himself were fifteen again!

'Mam, can I borrow your camera to take pictures of the deer?' Aidan asked.

'If you promise to take extra special care of it,' she conceded. 'And that means not climbing trees to photograph herons!'

'That gives me an idea,' Tubby exclaimed. 'Why don't we use the photos to illustrate articles on the wildlife here? You know the old saying: a picture is worth a thousand words.'

'Why don't we wait till tea is over to discuss your campaign?' Jakki smiled at Tubby's persistence. 'Who likes apple tart?'

Chapter 14

Aidan led Obhua and Iyabo along the path he and Margaret had taken to Crane Island. The lake was bustling with waterfowl and herons were clamouring in the treetops.

'Swan!' Obhua pointed to the white duck, which was swimming alongside some mallard drakes, coots and moorhens.

'That's a duck, silly!' Iyabo told him. 'The big bird over there is a swan.'

'Big swan, small swan!' Obhua shrugged. 'Aidan, why we no walk to the island?'

'It's too risky,' Aidan said. 'We'd sink in the mud. Do you hear the squawking? That's the young herons. Maybe if I climb one of those trees back there I'll be able to get a long-distance shot. Can you give me a leg up?'

Leaving Iyabo standing at the water's edge, Aidan and Obhua scaled a pine facing the island. From a branch near the top they had a good view, not just of the heronry but also of Park Field beyond. The green surface of the pasture had been torn off, leaving a raw, brown undulating landscape. There were four diggers visible: two yellow, one red and one orange, each of them scooping up bucketfuls of earth which they dropped into nearby trucks. When a digger's metal arm shook off its load of earth the grating noise drowned out the cries of the herons.

Looking through the viewfinder, Aidan saw that the red digger lined up with a nest in which a heron was feeding two fluffy young. Waiting till the shovel was directly above the mother bird, he pressed the shutter release. There! He'd got it! Next he took a shot of a heron sailing in like a kite to land expertly on a swaying branch, then of two chicks squabbling.

'Hi, Iyabo! We herons.' Obhua had risen to a half-standing position and, balancing precariously, was flapping his arms like wings.

'Sit down!' Iyabo signalled frantically.

'Yes, do!' Aidan concurred. 'You're spooking the herons.'

Once the boys were safely on the ground they all set out to find the deer. Aidan took a path that brought them close to Raheen Tower, which stood on the top of a hill and was used as a reservoir. When they approached the tower, however, they saw a tractor emerging from the farm buildings. Fearing that it might be Ray Kelly, Aidan beat a hasty retreat to the cover of the nearest trees.

'Why you in such a hurry?' Obhua complained after

catching his breath.

Aidan told them about the morning he and Darren had been chased by Kelly. 'Were you talking to Darren recently?' he added.

'Yes,' Obhua said. 'Friday he want to sell me hash but I not buy.'

'Did he say anything about Johnno?'

'Only that Johnno take care of you. I tell him Johnno, Clint, Shem and Marko bad guys but he don't care. He say, "They my friends".'

'He's a fool. Didn't he see what they did to you? Iyabo, will you try to make Darren see sense?'

Iyabo shook her head. 'Darren doesn't talk to any of the girls except Mandy – and she only talks to him when Clint's not around.'

'I thought I saw him talking to Margaret Murray yesterday during lunch.' Aidan hoped his voice sounded casual.

'Well, Margaret has other things on her mind,' Iyabo said archly.

'What things?'

'You know.'

'No, I don't.'

'Liar! She's always looking at you.'

'But she has a boyfriend already.'

'No, she doesn't. Blitzer's son writes to her but they're not – how do you say it? They're not engaged?'

'Going together.'

'Yes, they're not going together – just good friends.'

Something inside Aidan did a little somersault. Trying to sound casual he asked Iyabo, 'So, do you think I should write to her too?'

'Why ask me? In Nirambia the parents pick the person you will marry. It's the best way.'

'I marry Alicia Keys,' Obhua announced with a twinkle in his eye.

'Thanks for telling me about . . . you know who.' Aidan smiled ruefully at Iyabo. Just then a musical twittering sounded overhead, and looking up, he was surprised to see two swallows looping and weaving through the air. Surely this was a good omen.

'Look!' he pointed. 'The first swallows this year! Have you ever seen swallows in Nirambia?

'Yes,' Iyabo spoke while gazing upwards, 'those birds come back every dry season.'

'My cousin's family catch many swallow at Christmas,' Obhua said. 'When swallow come down to sleep in long grass, they hold up poles with sticky pieces of palm and swallow get stuck. Make delicious meal.'

Aidan was horrified but then he remembered Liam telling him how as a boy his father used to trap blackbirds and thrushes in winter and cook them on a griddle. Maybe Aidan's own father had eaten swallows in Nirambia.

As they went deeper into the leafy gloom of the wood, the raven began honking in the treetops but eventually he flew off. Taking a path marked with cloven hoof-prints, Aidan tiptoed forward and Iyabo and Obhua kept close behind. Presently they came to a spot where the path widened. Here speckled butterflies flitted about in the sunshine and birds warbled, chirruped and cooed. Under a great leafless oak, about ninety metres away, a number of stags were resting, their greyish-brown coats blending with the colour of the trunk and branches. Except for a few young ones, all of them had cast their antlers. Raising his camera slowly, Aidan got one good shot before the herd melted away through nearby trees.

'You'll have to give me that photo, Aidan,' Iyabo declared.

'I'll get a copy for each of you,' Aidan promised.

Following the direction taken by the stags they came to a freshly made clearing cluttered with oak branches. A yellow JCB stood near a pile of sawn trunks as if guarding them. Immediately Obhua ran forward and climbing into the cab, pretended he was driving.

'Get down from there,' Aidan said. 'Do you want Higgins to throw us out of the lodge?'

'Yes, Obhua, why are you always acting the fool?' Iyabo scolded.

Grinning impishly Obhua refused to budge. At that point, however, the sound of muffled tapping reached them. Signalling to Obhua to hurry after them, Aidan led Iyabo forward for about five minutes. Through a screen of hazels they saw Johnno chipping mortar from the demesne wall with a mallet and punch. Occasionally he stopped to glance furtively behind him or to drink from a bottle of Coke.

Aidan felt a shiver of nervous excitement run through his body. Whispering to Iyabo to wait with Obhua at the JCB, he took out his catapult and searching around, located a smooth pebble. Johnno's Coke bottle was placed on a log, not far from his right hand: it was a small target but not impossible. Drawing back the pan, Aidan took careful aim and fired. The pebble flew straight and true, shattering the bottle in pieces. Keeping a hazel between him and the startled vandal, Aidan retreated into the maze of trees. Behind him he could hear Johnno vowing vengeance but luckily he did not come charging in pursuit. Aidan smiled grimly: maybe this episode would make Johnno think twice before throwing rocks through windows!

That afternoon when she had returned from accompanying Iyabo and Obhua to the main gate, his mother questioned Aidan in Irish about climbing the tree and smashing the bottle.

'I trusted you, and you let me down,' she accused.

'So that's why you insisted on going with them to the gate!' Aidan's voice was shrill. 'You wanted to pump them for information. Thanks, Mam!'

'Never mind the sarcasm,' Jakki retorted. 'I asked you not to climb a tree and you disobeyed me. Then you put Iyabo and Obhua at risk by provoking Johnno. If you wanted to pay him back, you could have photographed him damaging the wall, whereas by firing the stone you were only descending to his level. Why don't you use your head? You didn't even take a photo of the JCB and that would have been evidence about the felling of the oaks. Now Johnno will do something terrible to us. I know in my heart he will.'

'No he won't, Mam, because he didn't see me,' Aidan assured her. 'And I can take a photo of the JCB anytime. I'm sorry about climbing the tree but when you get the film developed, you'll see it was worth it. You more or less promised Tubby you'd write articles on Cherryfield for *Gael Glas*, and my photos will be the icing on the cake.'

'You're very good at defending yourself,' Jakki smiled wanly, 'but, Aidan, you must learn to keep your promises and you must learn to avoid violence. If there's one lesson I learned from my stay in Nirambia it's that violence only breeds more violence – that's the reason I keep the mask.'

'Why?' Aidan was immediately curious. 'Has it something to do with my father?'

'I don't want to discuss it now – I've a splitting headache.' Jakki put her hand to her forehead. 'There's a lot of things I need to talk over with you about your –

about our family, but not just yet. This visit by Tom Keating has really flustered me – I don't know if I've a right to accept Senator Higgins's hospitality and then attack what he's doing. If only life weren't so damn complicated . . .'

'I don't care if Higgins is letting us stay here; he has no right to destroy Cherryfield for a stupid golf course,' Aidan told her. 'I hate his guts.'

'No, Aidan!' Jakki cried. 'If I thought I was responsible for making you think like that I'd never forgive myself. Senator Higgins may be misguided but he's not a bad man.'

Chapter 15

Despite the semi-darkness of nightfall half a dozen trucks with their headlights switched off were lumbering slowly and with much grating of gears through a gap in the demesne wall, guided only by the beam of a torch.

'Over this way, Red.' Johnno spoke into his mobile phone.

'You're sure we won't get stuck?' Red's voice crackled back.

'Not if you follow where the torch is pointing,' Johnno assured him.

'Just like a will-o'-the-wisp,' Red joked. 'All right, Sky Hawk, ease her— Shit!'

The trucks ground to a halt, their throbbing engines loud in the silence. The passenger door of the leading truck opened and a shadowy giant climbed down. Johnno picked his way over to him.

'Why didn't you clear the way properly?' Red growled as he shone a torch on the front wheel.

'What the hell did you expect?' Johnno retorted.

'I'm lucky to be alive. The whole bloody wall collapsed just as I was working on the last bit. If I hadn't stepped back in the nick of time I'd have been a gonner. And I had nobody—'

'Easy, man,' Red soothed. 'Just calm down.'

'Is it bad?' Johnno asked in a quieter voice.

'No sweat.' Red pulled a large stone to one side. 'I'm just a bit jumpy – we passed a patrol car outside Lisheen.' He squeezed Johnno's hand in a vigorous handshake. 'Most of my gang have gone back to their regular jobs so I hooked up with some New Age Travellers. They're new to this game but we'll soon break them in.'

'You didn't bring ecowarriors?' Johnno couldn't hide his disappointment.

'Look, man, we'll discuss that when the trucks are in off the road.' Red waved the drivers on, then he and Johnno led the way to the nearest clearing.

As the convoy crawled after the two bobbing torches, a ghostly white shape floated out from the pitch-black trees and circled the clearing erratically before floating back again.

'A barn owl!' Red exclaimed. 'That's an auspicious sign: she knows we're here to save her and— ' He broke off as the headlights of a car lit up the clearing.

'Cops!' Johnno cried, taking to his heels.

Darren lay on a foul-smelling mattress, staring at the

whitewashed wall, which was barely visible in the surrounding darkness. The mattress was placed on a concrete bench in the holding cell of Lisheen Garda Station. Apart from a coarse blanket there were no bedclothes. The cell had no windows and the toilet consisted of a bowl without a seat. The only light came from a small opening in the metal door through which Garda Sheila Gately had earlier handed him a cup of tea. He was trapped like a rat in a cellar and it was all because of his own stupidity.

Johnno had accused him of spilling the beans to Tubby about his plans for Cherryfield. The more he had denied it the more Johnno had insisted he was a liar. To make amends he had to promise Johnno that he would sell E to the college students that Saturday. He had flogged almost half of them outside the Castle Hotel when a patrol car came zooming round the corner and out jumped that git Morrison and his partner, Sheila Gately. They had collared him and frog-marched him to the station, where, after he had kicked Morrison in the shin in an attempt to escape, they took his name and address. When they phoned his mother and Youssou they weren't home, so he had been thrown in the cell to await their arrival.

He didn't like to think about what would happen when they arrived. His mother would go into one of her fits, accusing him of having brought shame on the family. She wouldn't think of how she herself had brought shame on it by taking up with a man less than a year after Doug was killed in a car crash.

Unlike his older brother, Dave, who now attended Hollybrook College in Kilbride as a day student, he hadn't objected when his mother started going out with Doug just a few years after their father died. At least Doug was Irish but Youssou was just a refugee. Oh, he was nice enough and he had been an engineer in his own country but in Ireland he could only get work as a doorman. Even Darren's sister, Emma, was embarrassed when girls in her class slagged her about her mother's boyfriend. That was nothing to what he had to endure from those three apes, Clint, Shem and Marko.

Nobody understood what it was like to be the only person in the school with a Black stepfather – not that Youssou was his stepfather yet. Maybe it would be better if he were – no, it wouldn't! Even if people didn't say anything, they would look at him with knowing eyes: poor Darren! Imagine having an African for a stepfather! But what were they thinking now? Poor Darren! His mother must be a right slut! Oh, God, he didn't mean that! He loved his mother and he didn't hate Youssou. It was all so confusing.

Why couldn't he be left alone instead of having Johnno and Clint and Blitzer and the cops dumping on him at every turn? He hadn't wanted to sell drugs. Now Johnno would demand the full price of the E and he wouldn't be able to pay him. Oh God, if only he could die this minute it would make everyone happy. He was a loser and he would never amount to anything.

Aidan and even Obhua had dropped him since he began hanging out with Johnno's gang. Well, to hell with them! If they felt like that, they weren't his friends to begin with. Imagine Obhua giving him the brush-off – as if somebody who had probably come into the country in a container truck was superior to somebody who had been born and bred here. He wouldn't be surprised if it was Obhua who had snitched on him to Johnno's pals after they dunked him in the toilet. Now that he thought of it, the three apes were on the hop the day Tubby was discussing Cherryfield. What had come over him that he had told Tubby that Johnno was going to save the demesne? Was it to impress the old know-all?

The grating of the key in the lock interrupted his thoughts. Garda Morrison switched on the light, almost blinding him, then led him out to the front room, where Sheila Gately was talking to his mother and Youssou. To his surprise his mother didn't fly off the handle. Instead she looked at him with a hurt expression, while Youssou held her arm as if to support her.

Sheila Gately suggested that they all sit while Garda Morrison wrote down the details. Garda Morrison then said that Darren had landed himself in a lot of hot water but if he was prepared to cooperate, he personally would see that the matter went no further. Who had supplied him with the ecstasy?

When Darren refused to answer, his mother pleaded with him to tell them everything he knew. People who got boys like him to peddle drugs were just scum. She had brought him up to do right and now he was disgracing her and his family by acting like a criminal.

'Your mother is right, Darren,' Youssou boomed in his deep African voice. 'You don't want to be sent to prison.'

'Don't I?' Darren shrugged.

'You'd be well advised to listen to your mother and Youssou,' Sheila admonished. 'They want what's best for you.'

'No, they don't!' Darren retorted. 'They don't give a damn what happens to me as long as it doesn't affect them.'

'That's not true.' His mother seemed on the point of tears. 'We love you very much.'

When Darren said nothing, Garda Morrison told him that he would be a fool to get a criminal record just to shield the likes of Johnno Cox. Oh yes, they knew full well that it was Cox who was his supplier, just as they knew he was behind the theft of Mr Neary's car and the breaking of the demesne wall to let the ecowarriors in. If he cooperated with them they would see that Johnno was taken out of circulation for a very long time.

Darren remained tight-lipped. Did Morrison think he

was an eejit? Who would protect him when Johnno was released from jail in a year or two? Not the guards, that was for sure.

'All right then,' Morrison lost patience, 'if you don't want to come clean there's nothing we can do except charge you with possession and sale of illegal drugs.'

On hearing this, his mother burst out crying.

'Now, look what you've done,' Youssou accused. 'You've made your mother's heart break.'

'Why can't you just leave me alone?' Darren cried. 'I didn't ask you to come here. I can take care of myself.'

'If getting caught selling ecstasy tablets is taking care of yourself then you aren't doing a very good job, are you, Darren?' Sheila pointed out gently. 'You know, your teachers said that up to this year you were a good student who never got into trouble, then recently you began to hang out with the wrong people. Now you've come to the big divide. If Garda Morrison completes this form you'll have to appear before Judge Mooney, who may well decide to send you to St Patrick's Institution for Young Offenders. Surely you don't want that?'

'I don't care,' Darren said hotly. 'I'm not a snitch.'

'It was only because I was such an eejit . . . and you looked so delicious . . . and I . . . I . . . —' Aidan was seated at his table in the sitting room of the lodge making another attempt to compose a letter. Just when he was on the point of giving up he decided to write in Irish. To his delight the opening salutation, '*A Mhairéad, a chara,*' seemed to free his thoughts. Quickly he dashed off a short note, which roughly translated as follows:

> *Dear Margaret,*
> *I often think of the day you came here and we visited the lake and went for a walk in the woods. You were able to spot so many things that I missed. I'm sorry if I acted out of turn. You looked so cool that I suppose I got carried away. Anyway, if I knew you would have been upset I would never have been so stupid. Do you think you can forgive me?*
>
> *Written in hope,*
> *Aidan.*

Chapter 16

In the ornate Indian Room in Cherryfield House, adorned with oil paintings of tiger hunts and polo matches, Senator Higgins sat at his desk trying to control his vexation. First there had been the awful moment when Ray Kelly had phoned to say that New Age Travellers had invaded his property, then there had been his galling failure to get the weirdoes ejected – the guards had explained that it would require a court order – and in the meantime the newspapers were having a field day. Even that rag the *Lisheen Leader* had the audacity to publish photos of the unwashed intruders, surrounded by their hens, goats and whippet hounds, setting up camp in a clearing intended for one of his chalets. What sort of a country was it when lawless dropouts could frustrate a major development that would put Lisheen on the map?

There was also an article by some hack who called herself 'Gráinne' claiming that the Travellers were defending Cherryfield from his vandalism – no mention whatsoever of the gap knocked in the demesne wall and the filth and litter created by the same people. Was it possible that Gráinne was (Oh no!) his own daughter? The writer had obviously first-hand knowledge of what was going on and she had a way of twisting things that reminded him of his clashes with Jakki over her behaviour with that Nirambian fellow in Trinity.

Still, he was probably being paranoiac. Surely Jakki wouldn't bite the hand that was feeding her a second time? She had, according to Timmy Keane, succeeded beyond all expectations in winning the respect of the staff in Lisheen Post Primary – not that that was surprising. Hadn't he himself always boasted that she had brains to burn? And she had a personality that could charm the birds out of the trees – provided she got her own way! That was the snag, her damn stubbornness. Almost every day he had to force himself not to visit the lodge, settling instead for the cold comfort of an occasional glimpse through binoculars of her or the boy (His grandson? No. Never!) walking by the lake or crossing the weir bridge. This estrangement was one of the hardest things he had ever endured, harder almost than watching his wife, Joanne, succumb to cancer, but years of playing the stock market had taught him the importance of timing. When the right moment to act came, he would seize it, come hell or high water. In the meantime he had to find some way to speed up the ejection of those . . . those troglodytes!

Picking up the phone, he was in the midst of dialling

his solicitor when his elderly housekeeper, Mrs McShane, came shuffling in to announce the arrival of a visitor. Senator Higgins signalled to her to wait till he had completed his call before sending the visitor in. Five minutes later he was greeting Jakki with a wary hello, his face revealing no trace of his surprise. God, but she was attractive, the spitting image of Joanne! If only she didn't look so intense . . .

To control her nervousness, Jakki came right to the point: 'Senator Higgins, I'm here to ask you not to build the chalets. The golf course is bad enough but those chalets will tear the heart out of Cherryfield. For the sake of your own reputation, please call a halt at once.'

'Hold it!' Senator Higgins raised his hand like a policeman. 'There's no need to address me like a stranger – I *am* your father.'

'If you don't mind, I'd prefer to keep this meeting on a business footing.' Jakki was unrelenting. 'We can discuss personal matters some other time.'

'Fine, if that's what you want, Miss Hannon.' He tried to conceal his hurt under a show of formality. 'But before you start lecturing me on my misdeeds, perhaps you could tell me if you're the writer of this libellous article?' He held up the *Leader,* where above a photo of prostrate oaks a headline screamed, 'THE PRICE OF PROGRESS?'

'What if I did?' Jakki retorted. 'All right, I had intended

to warn you first but the editor jumped the gun. Nevertheless, I stand by what I wrote.'

'*Quod scripsi, scripsi*: what I have written, I have written,' her father mocked.

Jakki could have clawed that smug, inscrutable face. 'You won't deny that you intend to build over a hundred chalets in the woods?'

'I have no intention of justifying my actions to you, Miss Hannon.' Her father remained unruffled. 'I would point out, however, that you and your son are guests in Cherryfield, given full use of the lodge without paying one penny in rent – not that I begrudge you its use. It has even been brought to my notice that you have visitors there on a regular basis.'

'Here, I've brought you a month's rent – and I'll pay every cent of back rent as soon as I'm in a position to do so.' She threw a handful of notes on the table.

For a moment it looked as if anger and pity would overwhelm her father but he regained his composure and pushed the money away. 'There's no need to do that,' he said. 'I should be paying you for keeping the lodge heated. In fact, why don't I give you a monthly fuel allowance? Here take this.' He began reaching for his wallet.'

'Don't!' she cried. 'I'm not some politician to be bought off.'

The look of pain on her father's face would have

melted a harder heart than Jakki's but when she remembered how he had turned his back on her and Aidan when they needed him most she was merciless.

'I didn't come here to insult you,' she said. 'Perhaps you mean well but cutting down trees won't help your image, not after the allegations of offshore bank accounts and the mysterious way you got Cherryfield rezoned. All right, it's too late to do anything about the golf course but why build the chalets? Surely there's some better way to raise money?'

'You're a witch!' her father gasped. 'How dare you rake up those slanders? Don't you realise two can play the same game? Why did your mother get cancer? Did it ever occur to you that it might have been brought on by stress, the stress caused by her only daughter's rebellion? How often did you visit her in hospital, when she was crying out for a visit from the one human being that she most longed to see? Why was your partner murdered in Nirambia? You don't find those questions very amusing, do you?'

Jakki turned deathly pale. 'All right, Senator Higgins,' she whispered, 'we both have things we'd rather not think about. I didn't come here to threaten but to plead with you not to destroy Cherryfield – if only for Aidan's sake.'

'And how is the boy?' Her father's expression softened. 'He seems a sturdy young fellow.'

'He's doing fine, all things considered.' Jakki tried to

compose herself. 'I let him invite friends home to keep him away from the town's troublemakers. We speak Irish to each other.'

'Can't he speak English?' Her father looked puzzled.

'Of course.' Jakki searched his face for any resemblance to Aidan: they had, she fancied, the same firm jaw and chin. 'The visitors you heard about are two Nirambian pupils from the Post Primary, Obhua and Iyabo. They come over at weekends – I feel it's important that Aidan be aware of his dual heritage. They're nice children and to them he's like one of their tree spirits, somebody who can teach them all about the wild creatures of the woods.'

'I know what you're thinking,' her father's voice was guarded. 'Nevertheless, the chalets will have to be built. It's that or go bankrupt.'

You looked so lovely that I suppose I got . . . Margaret was reading Aidan's letter, which Iyabo had handed to her in the resource area after History class.

'What does he say?' Iyabo stood on tiptoe to peer over her shoulder at the Gaelic script.

'Oh, just the usual stuff.' Margaret tried to sound nonchalant then she relented. 'He wants me to forgive him! Oh, if only he knew, Iyabo.'

'Knew what?' Iyabo demanded. 'That you wanted him to kiss you?'

'Yes,' Margaret admitted. 'But don't you dare tell him.

Oh, Iyabo, I'm so . . . so happy! I feel I could explode! When he touched my face that time I wanted him to kiss me but I was so confused. It was our first time out together and he took me by surprise. You know what I mean, don't you?'

'Yes,' Iyabo said. 'If a boy tried to kiss me I would box his ears – at least I think I would. Look! There he is now with Obhua. Let's stroll by and see what happens.'

When the doorbell rang Blitzer was correcting a maths test with one eye on the television, where a group of po-faced experts were discussing the rise in teenage homelessness. Grumbling to himself, he opened the front door. It was Tadhg Higgins, rain dripping from his expensive trilby hat and Burberry coat.

'Yes?' He didn't try to hide his surprise.

'Hello, Councillor.' Mr Higgins gave him a guarded smile. 'If you can spare a few minutes, there's something important I'd like to discuss.'

'Come in.' Blitzer led the way into the book-cluttered lounge, which was heated by a glowing briquette fire. 'You can leave your overcoat and hat on that chair. My wife is out with her I.C.A. pals. Can I offer you a drink?'

After a glass of Jameson and some uneasy small talk, Mr Higgins came to the point. If the ecowarriors blocked the felling of trees for chalet sites, the golf course and hotel would have to be put on hold. That would mean a setback for the local economy. He was aware that Mick had his own problems with Compu-Tel – you could say that each of them was under siege: one from a multinational and the other from a group of misfits.

'What do you want me to do?' Blitzer wondered if it was Ray Kelly who had told the Squire about his troubles with Compu-Tel.

'I'm getting our man to put a motion before the council condemning the illegal occupation of the demesne, and, well, I'm hoping you'll support it.'

'And why should I support a motion put by your crowd?'

'This kind of lawless behaviour affects us all, so I'm looking for cross-party support. Your group can amend the motion if they wish.'

'You're asking me to help in the destruction of Cherryfield?'

'I'm asking you to save it. As a practical man you know that if my plans fail the demesne will end up as a maze of housing estates – especially if our friends on the left get their way.

'You mean you'd sell up?'

'It would be that or go bankrupt. I know we don't exactly see eye to eye, but the devil you know . . .'

'Just for argument's sake, if I were to agree to your request, would you guarantee that the people of Lisheen would always have free access?'

'Certainly – within the usual safety constraints. And one other thing. As you know, Lisheen gatehouse is presently vacant: I can let you and your family have it on a life-long lease for a nominal sum.'

'That sounds like a bribe.'

'Not at all. The gatehouse was, I'm told, designed by Cassels. It's in good shape and if you and your family were to move in, you'd be preserving an important historic building for the community.'

'And people would accuse me of compromising my principles.'

'Maybe some would. But you and I know that in the real world we all have to compromise – if we didn't in politics we wouldn't even get a road sign erected. It's only young people and those idealistic Green fools that want everything perfect. Anyway, why don't you sleep on it and let me know your decision. This card has my mobile number.'

'And you'd give locals priority when it came to employing hotel staff?'

'You have my word.'

'I'll think about it.'

Chapter 17

In a clearing in the woods, Johnno sat on a felled tree beside a tall, bearded man of about thirty, whose hair was plaited in dreadlocks and whose lower lip and ears were adorned with gleaming metal studs. Beside them an open-sided, canvas-covered truck filled with various domestic animals, including a goat and two kids, looked like a modern version of Noah's ark. Four or five similar trucks and a camper van were parked haphazardly about the clearing. Women with plaited hair and voluminous dresses, children in ill-fitting clothes accompanied by whippet hounds and leather-clad men with untrimmed beards moved around a central fire or helped in the construction of a chicken pen. Were it not for the trucks and the pervasive aroma of cannabis smoke, one might have assumed that this was an ancient Celtic encampment.

'When do you reckon the squire will show up?' Red, the henna-haired warrior, absent-mindedly chopped off a branch stub with his axe.

'Search me.' Johnno took a long drag on a joint before

passing it to Red. 'All I know is that he goes for a ride through the woods about this time every day. The old git nearly caught me last Friday working on the wall. What will you do if he brings the cops?'

'It doesn't matter, friend.' Red blew smoke through his strong, yellow teeth. 'We've rigged up shelters in the tree tops. They're over there in those oaks, with rope bridges between them. If they knock one tree, we just move across to another. Have you a head for heights?'

'Not really,' Johnno admitted. 'But I'd be prepared to give it a go. How will you get food up to the shelters if the cops move in?'

'We'll hump up supplies beforehand.' Red tapped his nose. 'Me and Sky Hawk – the good-looking bird hugging that oak – have laid in enough muesli and water already to last a week.'

'Why is she hugging the tree?' Johnno gazed fascinated at a supple, jean-clad girl with her arms about an oak and her cheek resting against the bark.

'It's to absorb the tree's energy,' Red told him. 'Trees have spirits, just like you and me – that's why we hold mourning rites when a tree is cut down – and the tree's spirit can renew ours. Do you know that the druids used to cut mistletoe growing on an oak tree as a heal-all because they reckoned that in wintertime the oak's spirit energy passes into the mistletoe, which is still green?'

'No, I didn't.' Johnno looked bemused.

'Ah, you've a lot to learn, man,' Red grinned. 'By the way, we had a visitor this morning when we were aloft, a big lad – I reckon he could be anything from thirteen to fifteen. Man, could he climb!'

'Was he black?' Johnno was excited.

'I reckon you could say so.' Red scratched his beard. 'Is that significant?'

'If it's who I think it was, it sure is,' Johnno declared. 'That bloke nearly took my eye out with a catapult when I was working on the wall. He's Aidan Hannon from the lodge beside the lake and a right git. What did he want?'

'He wanted to know if we'd seen a white duck.'

'Well, he won't set eyes on her again. Last night me and a mate of mine, Clint, had roast duck for our supper.'

'How did you catch her?'

'A baited hook. We put a piece of bread on an eel hook and when she gobbled it we hauled her in and wrung her neck.'

'Man, that's cruel!'

'Why? People kill ducks and chickens every day and they shoot wild ducks.'

'Maybe, but not in the nesting season. You'd better pray Aidan doesn't find out.'

'You don't think I'm scared of that wuss?'

'He struck me as a fearless lad,' Red remarked. 'Anyway, he's on our side and from now on we need all the support we can get.'

'Not from the likes of him.' Johnno spat. 'His mother is a stuck-up cow who moved into the lodge about four months ago. Herself and Aidan go around talking Irish – I give you my solemn oath, Irish! She listens to weird music by candlelight and the two of them entertain darkies. Once their kitchen window was slightly open and when I peeped in, I saw this weird African mask on the sideboard with great white eyes and massive teeth. Can you beat that?'

'Hey, man, that's real cool,' Red enthused. 'They could be into juju – you know, that West African witchcraft.'

'You might have something there.' Johnno nodded as he considered this possibility. 'Do you reckon— wait! Here she comes now!'

They gazed in astonishment as Jakki picked her way through broken branches at the edge of the clearing. She was dressed in a black windcheater and jeans and her loose black hair glistened in the sun. But what really drew their attention was the camera she was carrying.

'Hey, lady, no photos!' Springing up, Red advanced on Jakki as she raised the camera to her eye. Before he could demand an explanation, however, a deep thudding warned him of an approaching vehicle and he turned aside to confront the new threat.

In through an opening in the oak trees came a tractor-towed slurry spreader, which halted menacingly on the outskirts of the encampment, its engine idling and its back towards them. Behind the tractor half a dozen workmen in yellow plastic jackets, armed with dung forks, formed a line. Red strode towards the intruders, the axe dangling from his right hand.

Early that morning, after a sleepless night, Jakki had dragged herself out of bed. The giant spiders were back; hiding in the corner, ready to pounce as soon as she lost consciousness. To distract her mind she had reviewed over and over her meeting with her father. Despite her secret hope that he would make some gesture to heal the rift between them, he hadn't abandoned the harsh stance she remembered so well. All that talk about going bankrupt was just so much rubbish – as if she didn't know he had plenty of untapped assets such as his corn mill in Lisheen and parcels of land in Dublin South. Mick Neary had alleged that 'the Squire' had a fortune salted away in a secret account in the Cayman Islands and Tom Keating had told her that there was a company set up to finance the golf course, with shares selling for as much as twenty thousand euro each.

Why hadn't she played the one card that might stop him cutting down the woods, his blood tie to Aidan? Senator Higgins, she should have said, which is more important to you, this son of mine, who, like it or not, is your direct descendant, or your precious chalets? But she had been so upset by his references to her past behaviour

– references that were really unfair – that she had let the opportunity pass.

When she shuffled in to the kitchen she had found Aidan's cereal bowl still on the dresser. That wasn't unusual but on this particular morning she feared that something was wrong. The bark mask watched her through empty white eyes much as it had on that awful day Maurice was murdered. Above it on the wall photos she had recently taken – colour shots of Iyabo pointing to a deer, Aidan and Margaret sitting on a high branch, Obhua feeding the wild ducks, the four young people examining a thrush's nest – seemed like fragile blossoms that the first breeze would scatter.

After a brief search, she found Aidan by the lake, gazing at a small mound of white feathers. There was no sign of the white duck. Though they didn't find paw marks, they decided that a fox was responsible. Her mind dark with foreboding, she preceded Aidan back to the lodge. Then when they had eaten breakfast he disappeared again. Reloading her camera, she set out for the clearing, where he had probably gone. With any luck she might get a few shots that would make her father regret his decision to forge ahead with the chalets.

Approaching the encampment, Jakki glimpsed Ray Kelly glaring at the ecowarriors through the back of a tractor cab window. He was reversing the slurry spreader towards them! She hurried to focus her camera, ignoring the red-haired warrior who seemed to be shouting something to her. A picture like this on the front page of the *Lisheen Leader* or, better still, *The Irish Times*, would truly be worth a thousand words. Suddenly a massive jet of stinking slurry spraying out from the tail of the spreader forced the big man to retreat but not before some of the liquid found its mark.

In a frenzy of excitement she clicked away: a shot of Johnno jumping up to scream profanities, of women grabbing children, of dripping dogs yelping in alarm, of wild-looking men bundling chairs, tables and utensils into trucks – and then the wind was carrying a fountain of spray in her own direction so that the viewer screen fogged over and a stench of liquid cow manure almost made her vomit.

Chapter 18

As Blitzer drove to school in his battered Toyota he had much to ponder. At three in the morning a crowd of drunken yobbos – almost certainly Johnno and his sidekicks – had wheeled a large wooden drum left by electrical workers at Compu-Tel into his garage door. His wife had become hysterical, vowing that if he didn't sell out at once she was going back to New York, where she had grown up and which, compared to Ireland, was a paradise. Wasn't all this a sign that he should accept Tadhg Higgins's offer of the gatehouse? With the nominal rent and the half million he would get from Compu-Tel for his bungalow, he would be in clover.

The only trouble was that he might be accused of sacrificing his principles for his own advantage, accepting largesse from a multinational company and an Irish tycoon. Still, he wouldn't really be selling out to the plutocrats since it was he who had insisted on the public's right of access to Cherryfield and that local workers be given first preference when it came to employing staff in the hotel.

Anyway, with the golf course half completed there was

little point in carrying on the fight to keep Cherryfield intact. Not that that fool Tom Keating would agree: he was all for joining the ecowarriors in their crazy campaign – as if a few dropouts living in the treetops would make Tadhg Higgins change course. Keating would be better advised to support the teachers' one-day strikes for decent pay and working conditions instead of writing windy articles and hobnobbing with that jailbird, John Cox.

During the first period Blitzer found Class 3D fairly subdued. To his surprise, Campbell and his shaven-headed buddies, Farrelly and McEvoy, had attempted some homework, while Hannon was so enthralled by Margaret Murray's smile, he seemed unaware that he was being asked a question.

'Aidan, I realise that in springtime a young man's fancy turns to thoughts of love but could you possibly turn your thoughts to the beauty of inverse proportion?' Blitzer was pleased when Margaret blushed at his sally – even if his own son, Ben, fancied her, these teenage romances only diverted students from their studies.

An imp like Obhua certainly didn't need romance to divert him. Today he was up to his usual tricks, reading a magazine article about The Rock, the American wrestler, and throwing sweets at other students. When Blitzer told him to write a letter of apology, Obhua readily complied, handing up a scribbled copy page which read:

Dear Neary,
how are you, I hope you are fine, how is your family, I hope they all fine, I am sorry for disturb you class
bye for now, Obhua

Was the fellow being impertinent or was he simply unaware of the proper terminology? He had just decided to give him the benefit of the doubt when in walked Darren Byrne without so much as a word of apology and flopped down at his desk.

'Why are you late?' Blitzer demanded.

'I overslept.' Darren yawned for the amusement of the class.

'Sir,' Blitzer corrected. 'I overslept, sir.'

'Whatever.' Darren yawned again.

Controlling his temper, Blitzer said evenly, 'See me at the end of class, Master Byrne. And the rest of you, carry on with your work – yes, Miss O'Donovan, that includes you!'

'But I don't know how to do the stupid question,' Mandy protested. 'You never showed us.'

'Oh, yes I did.' Aware that the mood of rebellion was catching, Blitzer quickly worked out the problem on the blackboard. 'You see; it's easy. You just apply the KISS principle.'

'What's the KISS principle?' Mandy demanded.

'Keep it simple, stupid,' Clint shouted out.

'Silence, Master Campbell!' Blitzer warned as Mandy indignantly began packing her books away.

'Where do you think you're going?' Blitzer tried to conceal his unease.

'You called me stupid,' Mandy accused. 'I'm going to tell my mother and she'll be seeing Mr Keane.'

'If you choose to see an insult where none was intended, I can't be held responsible,' Blitzer remarked as she swept out the door.

At the end of the class he handed Darren a self-report form.

'I'm not going to fill that out.' Darren rose to follow the others out of the room.

'Sit down!' Blitzer closed the door.

'Let me out!' Darren's voice was threatening.

'When you've finished that report,' Blitzer insisted.

'Let me out!' Darren began pacing about, ventilating heavily, working himself into a rage, sizing-up his adversary.

'You know that if you refuse to comply, I'll have to report you to Mr Keane?' Blitzer stood his ground.

'Let me out!' Darren approached, eyes blazing, fists closed.

Realising that matters were getting out of control, Blitzer stepped aside. If he tried to restrain this fellow, he would be accused of assault. What had come over him anyway? He used to be a likeable student.

As if to prove the truth of the adage that it never rains but it pours, his Leaving Certs were hyper. When he entered the room after morning break he found some of them writing insults on the blackboard, others sprawled across desks, chatting and laughing, and the two class louts, Jim Mullooly, a.k.a. Muller, and Iggy MacDermott, a.k.a. Mack, wrestling on the floor.

'Please take out your books.' Blitzer kept his composure.

'Ah, sir, can't we have a free class?' Joe Doyle, a dishevelled joker with dyed golden hair, pleaded.

'Yes, sir,' came a chorus of voices. 'We're fed up studying.'

'What use is maths anyway?' Louise Hamilton – another messer – enquired.

'You tell that to the interviewer when you go looking for a job,' Blitzer smiled. Despite himself he couldn't help liking this bunch. They were so – what was their phrase? – off the wall.

'I'm going to be a hairdresser,' Louise pointed out.

'Ah, sir, she got you there!' Mack crowed.

At this point Jamie O'Brien, the class eccentric, began chanting a rap in which the name Darren was frequently sandwiched between profanities.

'What has Darren done to deserve the honour of being commemorated in song?' Blitzer enquired.

'Didn't you hear, sir?' Joe Doyle ignored the glares of Mack and Muller. 'He's going to court next week for selling drugs. Judge Mooney will crucify him – six months in the Joy!'

'Not if he spills the beans on his supplier,' Jamie shouted out. 'Isn't that right, sir?'

'If he does, he'll be dead meat,' Muller growled.

So that explained Byrne's defiance, Blitzer told himself. The young fool was in trouble up to his eyes.

'Did you write that article on Cherryfield?' Joe Doyle asked. 'The one about the ecowarriors.'

'No, I didn't,' Blitzer said. 'And now if you will all open your books at the chapter on Simpson's Rule, Chapter 8, we can learn how to find the area of a golf course.'

'Oh, that's funny, sir!' Joe gave a mock laugh. 'You should be on the stage.'

'You'll be on the stage – to the principal's office – if you don't get your books out!' Blitzer's eye twinkled.

'Do you want to hear my rap about Cherryfield?' Without waiting for permission, Jamie launched into a rapid-fire diatribe:

'We're the eco-junkies high in the branches smokin'

Defying the establishment and all their phoney cluckin'

Come and try to knock us down if you think you have the muscle

Darren is supplying us and you know the squire can't stop him . . .'

Chapter 19

From the gloom of the mall, Darren in full uniform – though with tie askew – watched the students trooping along the footpath on their way to school. He was slumped on the garden seat outside Jim's Homecare Centre, taking occasional sips from a bottle of Lucozade. This was his second week on the hop but so far Obhua had covered for him by telling Tubby he was sick. His sister, Emma, was starting to ask questions, however, and it would only be a matter of time before Tubby or Diggy, the vice principal, contacted his home. Then his mother would go mental and Youssou would lecture him on the importance of education.

What use was education if he was going to end up in jail for selling drugs? Oh, he could still squeal on Johnno but that would be suicide. Even when he had begged him to forget about the money he owed, Johnno had turned nasty, whipping out his flick knife and threatening to cut his throat. The most he would agree to was an arrangement whereby Darren could work off his debt by selling more E. It was that or end up floating in the canal.

With a heavy heart Darren fingered the small plastic bags in his coat pocket. Each held four tablets but with most people stone-broke after the weekend he didn't have a hope in hell of flogging them. What if Timmy Keane had already contacted Dixon, the school liaison officer, about his absences? Dixon was supposed to be a right bastard. Between him, his mother, his pretend father Youssou and Judge Mooney he'd be crucified. If only his real father hadn't died all those years ago . . .

To lift his mind out of the black, bottomless pit into which it was sinking, he popped an E into his mouth and washed it down with Lucozade. Preoccupied with this activity, he didn't notice Obhua entering by the side passage until the scuffle of runners behind him made him start.

'What you doing?' Obhua demanded.

'It's none of your damn business!' The realisation that Obhua was making himself late for school by coming to talk to him only made Darren furious. It was bad enough being lectured by Youssou without a refugee his own age joining in.

'I not leaving.' Obhua was becoming stubborn. 'I tired of lie to Tubby.'

'Then eff off!' Darren snarled. 'Go on! Get back to Africa where you belong.'

'You say that, I tell everybody you stay out of school to deal Es,' Obhua threatened.

'You bloody snitch!' Swift as lightning Darren hit Obhua across the head with the half-full Lucozade bottle. There was a dull crunch but the heavy glass didn't break. Obhua sank wordlessly to the ground, his forehead striking the tiles. Blood oozed from his scalp.

Overcome with panic, Darren raced out of the mall, colliding with a group of late students. Blindly he shouldered his way into the open and charged up the street. Now he would be wanted for murder . . .

At about the same time that Darren was fleeing from the mall Aidan was padding through the woods, carrying a backpack filled with bread, cheese, bananas and milk. He had skipped his P.E. class to carry out this mission. The pack was heavy so he was often obliged to rest, something that gave him an opportunity to inspect the scene around him. Before Margaret started taking walks with him he had been mainly aware of birds, animals and insects; now, conscious of her delight in such things, he loved to gaze at bluebells carpeting the shade, blossoms opening on a chestnut tree, a cuckoo-pint rising from the earth like a small, green flame.

He was admiring a wood anemone growing under a sycamore when he spotted an owl pellet. On looking up, he discovered a barn owl roosting in the bottom fork, not far above his head. Was it her dead chicks that Sky Hawk had discovered while investigating a hole in a felled oak?

This owl was so close that he could plainly see her closed eyes, pale gold wing and the grey specks on her white front. Standing motionless there, completely on his own, he became conscious simultaneously of the tree's massiveness, the mingled choir of bird song and insect hum, the watching sky and the dozing owl so that a feeling of joy, of oneness with the living, breathing earth engulfed him. If only he had brought the camera, he could make Margaret understand something of what he was experiencing. He had asked her to cycle down the road outside the demesne wall so that she could make an appearance near the breach at precisely 9.30. There was always a chance she mightn't turn up, in which case he would have to manage on his own. Better make tracks.

Turning away, he followed a leafy, meandering path that eventually brought him close to the northeast edge of the wood. This was the danger zone. Moving cautiously, he worked his way to within a dozen metres of a high wire fence erected around the encampment site. The canvas-covered trucks had long departed and the breach in the wall had been repaired. He could see a man with a shotgun leaning against a blue plastic cabin left outside the fence. When the man turned, Aidan recognised him: it was Ray Kelly's young assistant, Paul O'Neill! There was no sign of Margaret.

Keeping the trunk between him and O'Neill, he began to climb an oak, his backpack slowing him down.

At a height of about fifty feet, he moved carefully out along a branch to a fork. Here he paused to catch his breath while he figured out his next move. He could see the taut rope strung between the branch on which he sat and another growing from an oak within the fenced area, where the ecowarriors had built untidy shelters in various treetops. Once he ventured onto that rope he would be in full view of O'Neill. Why hadn't Margaret arrived? It was now 9.45 so the chances were she hadn't been able to get away. If only he could be sure that O'Neill just had the gun for show or that it was loaded with blanks. Well, desperate situations called for desperate measures: he would have to distract him.

Taking out his catapult, he fired a cone into briars growing beyond the plastic cabin. To his delight O'Neill, after looking around, began walking back to find out what had caused the sudden noise. And then it happened! There was Margaret standing like an acrobat on the nine-foot high demesne wall. O'Neill changed direction to approach her. Losing no time, Aidan made his move. Hooking his legs around the rope while hanging beneath it with the backpack's straps cutting into his shoulders, he quickly pulled himself across to the tree inside of the fence. Before he could get a foothold, however, O'Neill hearing the branches creak turned to stare. Immediately Aidan froze, his heart thumping painfully.

After what seemed an eternity O'Neill turned back to

question Margaret, and, releasing his legs, Aidan swung down to a branch beneath him. Losing no time, he climbed up to a rope bridge, which allowed him to walk easily to the first shelter. When he looked over at the wall Margaret had disappeared and O'Neill was returning to the plastic cabin. This was the last time he would attempt a crossing in daylight.

Red and Sky Hawk, both of whom exuded a mingled odour of sweat and hash, were overjoyed to see him, helping him to transfer the contents of his backpack to a wire-fronted larder, where it would be safe from magpies and squirrels. The canvas-roofed shelter had room for only two people, so while Aidan sat on a branch, Red asked what the Post Primary students were saying about them and their comrades.

'Some of them are behind you,' Aidan said. 'In fact, the girl that was over there on the wall, Margaret Murray, is organising a "Save Cherryfield" demonstration – but others think you're nutters,' On hearing this, Red laughed his hearty laugh.

'Well, that's all right,' Sky Hawk remarked. 'We've been called worse things. Here, this is for you.' She handed Aidan a tiny fawn she had whittled out of seasoned yew, explaining that the yew was one of Ireland's five magical trees.

Aidan accepted the gift gratefully, asking if she would mind if he gave it to his girlfriend. 'Certainly. I'd be flattered,' Sky Hawk assured him and then asked him to tell them all about the lucky damsel. 'Oh, go on,' she pleaded when he seemed reluctant to comply. 'That big lug used to give me presents once – it won't hurt him to be reminded of our courting days.'

'See, Aidan,' Red grinned good humouredly, 'that's how girlfriends turn out!'

Aidan's halting description of how he had written to Margaret and how she had responded to his letter was cut short by the arrival of Johnno, who, bleary-eyed and dishevelled, came gingerly along the rope bridge from an adjacent tree. Immediately Aidan rose, hiding the fawn in his trousers pocket.

'Chill out, Coco Pops,' Johnno drawled. 'Nobody's going to rob you.'

'Who are you calling Coco Pops, you lousy psycho?' Aidan flared up.

'Don't mind him, Aidan,' Red advised. 'It's just that the swaying of the treetop keeps rookies awake at night.'

'Is that so?' Johnno retorted. 'Well, if you want my help, you'd better give this git his walking papers. It's him or me.'

'Then I'm afraid it's you, man.' Red spoke quietly.

'Fine!' Johnno snarled with mingled hurt and rage. 'If you want your campaign to depend on the likes of that treacherous darky—'

Aidan made to lunge at his tormentor but Red

grabbed his jumper with one giant hand. It was well he did so because Johnno had his flick knife open.

'Put that away or somebody could get hurt,' Red might have been talking to a naughty child. 'And, Aidan, get into the shelter before you fall and break your neck.'

'You bloody ecowarriors wouldn't be here today, if I didn't send for you in the first place,' Johnno seethed, pocketing the knife. 'I risked my neck making the hole in the wall for you but you're no better than all the other bastards in this kip of a country – kick a man in the teeth when he tries to help you. Well, feck the lot of you!'

And saying this, Johnno lurched back along the swaying rope bridge.

Chapter 20

The next day was Wednesday, the middle of the school week. Blitzer sat bolt upright in his Toyota, which was parked opposite Cherryfield wall. He was half-listening to the morning news while keeping a close eye on the Lisheen road.

About twenty minutes previously he had passed Johnno slouching towards the village and on impulse had swung the car into Euromart and dialled Ray Kelly on his mobile. Now would be a good time to put into effect the plan they had discussed. Ray was willing to go along provided Blitzer acted as lookout. The upshot was that Blitzer had waited until Johnno passed Euromart then driven back towards Cherryfield, where he had turned the car around and switched off the engine.

In the rear-view mirror he saw Ray and Paul O'Neill emerge from the entrance to Cherryfield, each carrying a petrol can. After sighting his car they hurried across the road and into trees growing on the canal bank. Blitzer dialled Emer, the school secretary, to say that he would be late then reset the mobile at Ray's number; if he and Paul didn't act fast there was every chance that Johnno would return. What would happen if he spotted the Toyota? Well, he would hardly report him to the gardaí and even if he did Blitzer could always claim that the engine had overheated. Tough luck, Johnno!

Not that he had any qualms about what was taking place. For years he had endured this psychopath's campaign of vandalism and violence. He might forgive him for what he had done to him personally, even the attack with the screwdriver, but he would never forgive him for turning his wife into a nervous wreck who went to pieces every time she heard a noise outside the house. And then there was the damage he was doing to the youth of Lisheen with his drug dealing. Since the gardaí seemed powerless to curb him, he had approached Ray soon after Tadhg Higgins's visit with a view to taking direct action. If he was going to move his family to the gatehouse he couldn't have the likes of Johnno camped within a few hundred yards of their doorstep.

As the minutes dragged by, he went over in his mind what Ray had told him about seeing Johnno with the ecowarriors. It was true that he himself had campaigned to preserve Cherryfield but the TV pictures of a band of unwashed savages living in trees had opened his eyes. No wonder that Johnno had joined them – birds of a feather! Well, the time for decent people to fight back had come – though airy-fairy eggheads like Tom Keating might argue otherwise.

His thoughts were interrupted on noticing in the rear-view mirror a dark plume of smoke rising from the trees. He smiled grimly. Now Johnno would learn what it was like to be on the receiving end of vandalism. Waiting for what seemed an eternity till Ray and Paul emerged from the trees, he switched on the engine and raced back to school.

On reaching the town, Johnno had run into a crowd of retards from the college and Post Primary marching up Main Street behind a banner reading 'HALT THE RAPE OF CHERRYFIELD'. A lot of heed the likes of Squire Higgins would pay to their stupid carry-on! After selling E and hash to one of his college regulars, he had purchased a Chinese takeaway, a six-pack of beer and a slice of apple crumble. Now he was looking forward to sitting down in his shelter and having a feed.

As he turned in off the road to walk along by the canal he noticed smoke rising from trees beyond a bend. Had Travellers camped on the towpath? No, there was no sign of vans. If it was a tramp that had arrived, he would give him his marching orders: nobody was going to squat on his patch. When he had walked about eighty metres Johnno caught sight of something burning just below the spot where his shelter was located. What the feck— Breaking into a lope, he quickly drew near the fire then halted in dismay. Some gits, almost certainly Higgins's workmen, had flung his shelter – poles, carpets, plywood sheets, the whole kit and caboodle – down onto the towpath, where they had stacked it in a heap and torched it. They had even left the empty petrol cans. The only items they had spared were his sleeping bag, blankets and CD player.

He stood there immobile, letting the full horror of the situation sink in. If the bastards who had done this had been thrown into prison, then kicked out of their own homes, and turned away by a bunch of eco freaks, they might have thought twice about leaving somebody without a roof over his head. You wouldn't treat a dog like this, let alone another human being. Tears welled in his eyes, but instead of crying he let out a short anguished howl such as a wounded animal might make. Gradually anger replaced his dismay. He would make those feckers pay for their actions if it was the last thing he did.

He needed a joint to calm himself down. Luckily he always stashed his dope in a hole in a beech tree about ten metres from the shelter. When he checked the beech the gear was still secure. Quickly he rolled a joint then decided to eat his dinner and smoke afterwards. As he wolfed down the lukewarm chow mein while standing with his back to the fire, his eye lit on an old barge he had passed further down the canal. It might be rusty but at least it would be dry. He would check it out. Opening a can of beer, he drank it in a few prolonged gulps then lit the joint. By God he wasn't finished yet.

That afternoon Johnno lay on the deck of the barge, which was tied by a thick rope to a stake in the bank. His sleeping bag and blankets were folded into a bundle on which he rested his head and shoulders. Beside him were three or four beer cans and an empty cardboard box that bore traces of apple crumble. The barge had once been used to transport barrels of Guinness but the hold had been boarded over to provide a viewing deck for people taking sightseeing trips and metal guardrails had been added along the sides.

Across the canal cowslips grew in creamy patches on the flank of the railway, blackbirds and finches sang in the trees and a moorhen clucked in sallies at the edge of the water but Johnno did not notice. He was smoking a joint while listening to his CD player:

'Please Lord, this boy needs Jesus
Help this child, help him destroy these demons.'

Jaysus, that Eminem could tell it like it was, the hypocritical preacher pretending to be concerned about children and all the time the old bastard was preying on them. That was the sort of world it was, adults assuring you they had your best interests at heart and then they locked you up in a cell or burned the miserable roof over your head.

Despite the soothing effects of the joint, anger flared in him again as he recalled the sight that had met his eyes two hours previously. Tonight he would have to sleep on the barge – not that that would be a problem, given the fine weather. It was the rain that would cripple him. He would have to find some gaff in the village – maybe even ask Tubby for a spare room – but not before he had paid back the squire and his henchmen.

Paul O'Neill must have told the squire that he had seen him with Red so the squire had decided to teach him a lesson. Well, two could play at that game: an eye for an eye. He would burn down Cherryfield House – no, that would be too well guarded. The lodge? It was easy to reach and he would be killing two birds with one stone because Jakki was just as guilty as the squire. When the lodge went up in flames she and that darky son of hers would have something new to photograph.

His mind calmed by this decision, he allowed himself to drift into a fuddled haze from which he was aroused by chattering voices. A group of teenagers was approaching along the towpath. It didn't take him long to recognise the guffaws of Mack and Muller and the whinny of Nicola. Soon they, together with Clint Campbell, Steffi and Mandy, were crossing the plank laid between the grassy bank and the barge.

At first they couldn't believe that he had been burned out. How could anyone else have known where he had his shelter?

'That snitch Darren Byrne or Tubby could have told them,' Johnno pointed out. 'It could even have been Aidan Hannon – but that's enough about the darky. I'll deal with him in my own good time.'

'Where will you live now?' Nicola lit a joint.

'Who knows?' Johnno shrugged. 'Isn't it a queer state of affairs when Blacks can come into Lisheen and get their pick of houses and I haven't a roof over my head?'

'I thought you were going to live with the ecowarriors.' Mack broke open one of the cans of lager he had brought with him and handed it to Johnno.

'With those freaks?' Johnno spat. 'No, they're no good. Yesterday morning when Aidan saw me aloft at Red's shelter he got thick, so I told Red to get rid of him and that Judas said I was the one who would have to leave. The darky brings them food so they figure he's more useful than a bloke like me. Anyway, I was getting fed up with the whole circus. Another day in that magpie's nest would have driven me out of my bleedin' mind. And you know what? It's a lost cause: Squire Higgins has bought the *Lisheen Leader,* so there'll be no more articles about chalets. Money speaks louder than justice in this kip of a country.'

'We have news that will cheer you up,' Clint passed a joint to Mandy, 'Byrne crowned Obhua with a Lucozade bottle.' And he proceeded to give a dramatic account of the attack.

'Good for him,' Johnno commented. 'I reckon Byrne has more guts than I thought. Listen, why don't you, Mandy and Nicola go to see if any of my stuff was left near the shelter? I want to have a talk with Mack and Muller. And bring back the petrol cans,' he added.

When the others were out of earshot, Johnno broached his plan for burning the lodge.

'No way!' Mack protested. 'I'm not having anything to do with that kind of business.'

'You can count me out too,' Muller declared. 'It's one thing to sell E – but setting fire to a house? Man, that's crazy!'

'All right then,' Johnno used anger to conceal his hurt, 'both of you can feck off! Clint and me will do the job ourselves.'

'I promised me ma . . .' Mack left the explanation unfinished.

'Feck off before I knife you!' Johnno turned to gaze into the canal as the two hurried away. Sod them, the snivelling cowards!

He was still in the same position when Clint, carrying the petrol cans, returned with the girls.

'Where did Mack and Muller go?' Clint asked.

'They've gone home to their mammies.' Johnno hurled his empty lager can into the water. 'You and I—' He broke off at the sight of two figures approaching along the towpath.

'It's Darren's sister, Emma, and her stepfather!' Mandy quickly dropped her joint onto the deck and crushed it with her runner.

When the two came to where the barge was moored, Youssou asked if they had seen Darren.

'He didn't come home last night,' Emma broke in, 'and Mam is afraid that after what happened he may have . . . he may have . . . ' Her distress was clearly visible.

'He hasn't been around here.' Johnno let his eyes roam over her face and figure. She was a fine bird.

'Are you the gentleman they call Johnno?' Youssou enquired.

'So what if I am?' Johnno surveyed him insolently.

'You're the one who persuaded him to sell drugs,' Youssou spoke with quiet authority. 'Please don't trouble to deny it. If harm should come to that boy, you will be held responsible by me.'

'You can't come round here making wild accusations,' Johnno blustered. 'Did Darren say I made him sell drugs?'

'He didn't have to say it,' Youssou remained calm. 'Come, Emma, we'll walk to the lock.'

Johnno watched as they continued on their way. 'Bye-bye, you Black bastard,' he sneered, but not loud enough to be heard by Youssou.

Chapter 21

Because he had stopped to talk to Iyabo about the correct pronunciation of '*Gbe nuesoun*!' the Nirambian phrase for 'Shut up!' Tubby was late in reaching his customary table in the staff room. He had to squeeze in between Avril Brogan and Paul Duignan, who grumbled at having to move his chair. On the far side of the table Mick Neary and Timmy Keane, the principal, were engaged in a discussion about future industrial action with Phil Lynch, the year head for Third Years and union rep, who sat at the end of the table, tucking into a plate of salad.

'What kept you, Tom?' Avril paused in the act of spreading cream cheese on a slice of bread.

'I was brushing up on my Nirambian,' Tubby joked. 'It's a fascinating language. Do you know they use different forms of address when talking to children and adults, something like *tu* and *vous* in French? For example, if I were saying "Good morning" to you I would say "*E Káàárò* Avril", but if you were Iyabo I would say "*Káàárò* Iyabo", dropping the initial E.'

'Is that your piece of trivia for today?' Diggy sniffed. 'You didn't bother to find out how Obhua is doing, I suppose?'

'As a matter of fact, I did, Paul,' Tubby beamed. 'Iyabo said he's doing fine. He should be back with us on Monday. The hospital said he suffered only a slight concussion – though they did have to stitch up the head wound. Has anything been heard about Darren Byrne?'

'No,' Avril said. 'Emma told me the family is really upset. It seems that when he ran away before he always texted her on her mobile.'

'What's this I hear about you going into the B & B business, Tom?' Timmy Keane broke in on their conversation.

'Yes,' Blitzer piped up. 'Is it true you've taken in that outlaw, John Cox? I know you and he are working with the eco-freaks on the Cherryfield Campaign, but taking him into your house after what he did to me . . . Boy, you need to have your head examined!'

'It seems, Mick, that your friend Squire Higgins burned down his shelter,' Tubby removed the wrapping from his sandwiches, 'so I offered him the spare room till he can get back on his feet.'

'If you lie down with dogs, you'll rise up with fleas,' Blitzer remarked. 'And by the way, Senator Higgins is not my friend: I deal with him as I would with any member of the public.'

'You mean you tell him how much to put in the brown envelope!' Phil emitted a loud guffaw.

'Oh, so he's *Senator* Higgins now,' said Tubby, pouring himself a cup of tea. 'Apart from his wealth, is there that much difference between him and Johnno?'

'I don't think Higgins has been sent to St Pat's for selling drugs and breaking and entering,' Timmy pointed out.

'No, but he probably has done more harm to the country than Johnno will ever do.' Phil cut a tomato into small pieces. 'People like him make fortunes out of crooked business deals and getting land rezoned and then put their ill-gotten gains into offshore bank accounts so they won't have to pay taxes, while poor suckers like you and me have to go on strike for a few lousy quid extra a month.'

'Let's forget the left-wing rhetoric and get back to Keating's house guest.' Timmy's eyes had a wicked gleam. 'Aren't you aware that the guards have him pegged for supplying Byrne with the drugs he was selling?'

'I thought a man was innocent until proven guilty.' Tubby put more sugar in his tea.

'Innocent my foot!' Timmy snorted. 'Cox is an evil git who's done more to corrupt the teenagers of this town than any person I know.'

'They don't need much encouragement,' Tubby remarked. 'Fellows like Clint Campbell could teach Cox a lesson or two. I'm not saying Johnno is an angel but if you don't give young offenders a chance to get back on their feet, you're condemning them to a life of crime.'

'Well said,' Phil applauded. 'Crime is a symptom of a sick society.'

Their conversation was interrupted by the arrival of Maureen Friel, who sat at the end of the table, next to Avril.

'Did you see the photo of Darren Byrne?' Maureen handed round the *Lisheen Leader*. 'They're asking anyone who has seen him to contact his parents or the gardaí.'

'We all know about that.' Diggy turned the pages. 'Is there any article by Diarmaid? What happened, Tom? Has your inspiration dried up?'

'No, it hasn't,' Tubby replied. 'If you care to read *Gael Glas* you'll find an updated account of the rape of Cherryfield, complete with photos of felled trees and bulldozers.'

'Who reads that green rag?' Diggy scoffed.

'At least it's an honest rag, not a mouthpiece for Squire Higgins's hacks like the *Leader*.' Tubby sipped his tea.

'Is it true that the ecowarriors are being helped by that son of Jakki Hannon's?' Blitzer asked, offering Maureen some biscuits.

'His name is Aidan,' Tubby reminded him, 'and I'm not privy to what he does.'

'He's missed a fair few classes recently and when he's

in, he's more interested in exchanging adoring glances with Margaret Murray than in paying attention to his lessons,' Blitzer groused. 'Which reminds me: they're both absent today.'

'If you had a choice between Margaret Murray and maths when you were his age, which would you have gone for?' Phil Lynch demanded through a mouthful of lettuce.

'The maths will stand to him when the romance has faded.' Blitzer enjoyed their groans.

'Maureen, you teach Aidan,' Diggy said. 'Is he missing your classes?'

'Occasionally,' Maureen admitted. 'Yesterday, he and Margaret were at the "Save Cherryfield" protest. But he's still miles ahead of the rest of the class. When you hear him and Margaret gabbing away, you'd swear they were two Inishmaan teenagers.'

'I didn't realise they had Black teenagers in the Aran Islands,' Diggy joked.

'No,' Maureen agreed. 'And if they had, they'd call them blue. The Irish for a Black man is *fear gorm*.'

'That's probably because the first Africans our ancestors saw were Berbers or Arabs who painted themselves blue,' Timmy grinned. 'You see I'm a student of history too!'

'Why the emphasis on colour?' Avril reproved. 'Do you realise that we now have students from five continents, including Asia and South America? My Second Years are presently stretching strings on a map from Ireland to every country where one of our students was born, and you should see it: it looks like the rays of the sun.'

'The truth is we're a hybrid race,' Phil stated, 'a mixture of wave after wave of invaders and immigrants who ended up here because there wasn't enough room on the Eurasian land mass.'

'And they all originated in Africa a million or more years ago,' Tubby broke in. 'The only thing that makes us Irish is our culture. And by that definition, Aidan is more Irish than anyone sitting around this table, with the possible exception of Maureen.'

'Since when do you have to be fluent in Irish to be considered a true Irishman?' Blitzer objected.

'That's right,' Phil rowed in. 'By your definition Yeats or Joyce wouldn't qualify as Irish.'

'Or for that matter, neither would Keating,' Timmy delivered the knockout punch.

'Yes, Tom, how do you answer that?' Avril demanded.

'Leaving aside the matter of Irish,' ignoring a hail of protests from the table, Tubby changed tack, 'Aidan is one of the most promising young fellows we have in the school. In fact, I would regard him as the forerunner of the new breed of Irishman that's emerging – a good scholar and at the same time a foster child of nature, someone who's willing to fight to protect our environment.'

'Oh, ho!' Blitzer crowed. 'Back to the same old nature groove! If man hadn't altered nature, we'd all be going round in our pelts, eating nuts and berries instead of that ham and cheese sandwich you're devouring.'

'Mick, I'm shocked!' Maureen protested in mock horror. 'The idea of you running around in your pelt!'

'Well, maybe that would be better than polluting our air and rivers and cutting down our woods and turning our parklands into golf courses.' Tubby took another bite.

'You really are a Green fanatic,' Blitzer mocked.

'*Gbe nuesoun*!' Tubby wiped mayonnaise off his lips with a tissue.

Before Blitzer could respond, the secretary, Emer, looking very grave, approached and whispered something in Timmy's ear, whereupon Timmy rose and struck his empty cup with a spoon to gain the room's attention.

'I have something very sad to announce,' he told the hushed teachers. 'Darren Byrne's body has been found in the old church ruins in Fennor Cemetery. He was dead a number of days, probably from an overdose. Fennor is where his father is buried.'

During morning break that day Aidan and Margaret had borrowed bikes so that they could cycle to Cherryfield and photograph the red deer. It was Aidan's fifteenth birthday. The consciousness that they were taking a risk only added spice to the occasion: without a word being spoken both knew that they had other things on their minds. After getting a long-distance shot of hinds that were big with calf, they hurried back to the lodge.

'What'll we do now?' Margaret asked coyly once Aidan had closed the door.

'Come here and I'll show you!' Aidan made a grab for her but she dodged to one side and, giggling excitedly, raced round the kitchen table and into the sitting room.

'I'm acomin' in.' He put on the mask and growling like an ogre, strode after her, his runners thumping the floor. When he entered the sitting room, however, there was no sign of Margaret, so he stomped out into the narrow corridor. On his right there was the toilet and beside it the bathroom – but she would hardly hide there. On his left the corridor ran past facing doors opening into the bedroom and kitchen before ending at a blank wall. Since the only light came from the toilet window, the lower corridor was in semidarkness: that was where she would have headed.

'I'm agoin' to get you.' He tiptoed towards the bedroom. While he was gently turning the knob Margaret came flitting down the corridor from the bathroom and threw herself laughing on his back so that he lost his balance and they both went crashing into the end wall. There was a groan of yielding timber as the wall gave way, cushioning the impact.

Picking themselves up, they peered at the shadowy gap.

'Oh, Aidan, I didn't mean to— ' Margaret was mortified.

'It's all right,' he lied, knowing his mother would be furious. The air in the corridor was turning colder. Reaching out his arms, he drew her to him. 'We'll blame it on the mask.' He laid his cheek gently against hers.

She yielded for a moment, soft and fragrant; then kissing him swiftly on the mouth, she drew away.

'We'll have to do something about the wall,' she told him.

'Let's get a candle and see what the damage is.' He wondered if the mask was really responsible for this stroke of bad luck.

When they returned with a lighted candle the flame showed the mask lying undamaged on the floor, the empty white eyes gazing up at them, blank and inscrutable.

'Over here!' Margaret exclaimed. 'Quick!'

Aidan brought the candle to the gap in the wall and his eyes almost popped out of his head. Behind thick veils of cobwebs he could just make out stone steps leading downward. He needed a better look. When he pushed at the boards, there was a groan as of rusty hinges and an entire panel moved inward.

'It must be a secret chamber!' Margaret was bubbling with excitement.

'We'll soon find out.' Brushing aside the cobwebs, Aidan began gingerly to descend into the stale, tomblike depths. Margaret followed, with one hand resting on his shoulder. At the bottom step they found themselves facing a low, stone-lined tunnel.

'Do you think the air might be poisonous?' Margaret spoke in hushed tones.

'No,' Aidan tried to hide his own unease. 'The candle is burning okay.'

Taking her hand in his, he led the way into the tunnel, both of them stooping. A rat scurried into the shadows ahead but they pressed on till eventually they reached a small brick chamber, which was empty, except for pieces of fallen roof timber.

'This was probably a wine cellar – or it could have been used by Myler MacMorris to store arms,' Aidan said, recalling what his mother had told him.

'Oh, isn't it exciting!' Margaret whispered. 'He could have broken a hole in the roof if he was trying to escape from the redcoats.'

'You're right,' Aidan agreed. 'We must be fifty metres from the lodge, so that means we're under trees not far from the weir.'

'Isn't it chilly?' Margaret moved close to Aidan and he

pressed her to him with his left arm and kissed her upturned mouth while the candle threw their shadows like huge ghostly figures on the wall.

'We'd better get back to school before your mother returns.' She broke away, flustered.

'Yes,' he conceded. 'And we won't mention finding this or she'll know we were in the house while she was out.'

'What about Iyabo and Obhua?' she asked. 'Will we tell them?'

'Okay,' he took her hand to lead her out, 'we'll tell them but they'd better not blab to anyone else. It'll just be the four of us that know.'

Chapter 22

Jakki knelt with Aidan and Margaret near the end of a pew, trying to concentrate. The church was crowded with men, women and children but hardly any teenagers – though they would almost certainly be there in force tomorrow for Darren Byrne's funeral mass. Sunlight flooding through the stained-glass windows bathed the interior in multi-hued tints that reminded her of Nirambia. Nevertheless, if Mick Neary hadn't told her that there would be a West African priest visiting this Sunday she wouldn't have come because she was presently looking after Iyabo and her younger sister, Abosede.

Iyabo and Abosede's mother had been obliged to move to a new house down the country provided by the health board and in order not to interrupt the girls' education Mr Keane had begged her to take them in until the end of the school year. While she was pleased to brush up on her Nirambian, Jakki found the presence of two more people in the lodge disconcerting – not that she didn't like the girls; they were high-spirited, intelligent children but when Abosede and Aidan began chasing each other from room to room with Iyabo berating them for their misbehaviour, it was difficult to relax.

Last night she had slept badly, the presence of the girls in the next bed bringing back memories of her stay in Africa and Maurice's murder. Now, as if to continue the nightmare, Darren's coffin rested on a trestle near the side aisle. Had she been wrong to leave the girls sleeping in the lodge while she and Aidan went to Mass? No, they weren't Catholics and the rest would do them good. In the afternoon they could travel with Oluwaseun to the mosque in Dublin, while she and Obhua attended an evangelical church there. Still, she probably shouldn't have left them on their own. What if that fellow Johnno came prowling around? Oh, she would just have to stop this worrying.

Mick Neary was reading a bible passage about the Father sending the Paraclete and Jesus saying, 'I do not give you peace as the world gives it.' That was the secret of happiness, being at peace with yourself even though the world was falling to pieces around you. She had made great progress in the last few months, getting back to work, taking up photography and writing again, but, most of all, winning back Aidan's trust. There he was beside her with his beautiful, intelligent girlfriend, his eyes turned to the altar. Her heart swelled with pride as she glanced at him. Surely if she only counted her blessings she had every reason to be at peace?

Further back, on the other side of the aisle, Senator Higgins also gazed at the altar, his mind elsewhere. After a remark one day by Mrs McShane that she had seen Jakki in the church, he realised that these Sunday attendances could afford an occasional close-up view of his daughter and . . . that boy of hers. He had many reasons to feel at peace: the golf course was coming in on schedule; the ecowarriors had been, if not ejected, at least contained; and with his purchase of the *Lisheen Leader* the negative publicity had ended, but despite all this he felt dissatisfied. What was the use of creating a world-class golf course if he had no one to succeed him? And, yet, he had a grandson— No, he would never accept that . . . or would he?

His thoughts drifted to the time when he had first learned that his beautiful eighteen-year-old daughter was pregnant and, worse still, by an African. His world had collapsed at that instant. All the plans that he and Joanne had made for her were swept away by her irresponsible and thoughtless behaviour. She had been so adorable when she was growing up that he had probably spoiled her, but Trinity had changed her too – all that liberal nonsense about people of different races being essentially the same! But what was past was past. No use in crying over spilt milk. He hadn't meant to send her away resentful when she called on him in the Indian Room. What a bittersweet encounter that had been, a botched attempt to restore something that years of estrangement had marred. Was it irrevocably destroyed? If only she could have understood the economic realities that tied his hands in regard to Cherryfield. But no, she was too blinkered by her liberal preconceptions: money was the root of every evil, therefore those who created wealth had to be corrupt. You'd think that by now life would have taught her that the truth wasn't quite so simple. Without wealth, there would have been no great art or architecture, no Cherryfields.

A distinct '*Fáinleoga*! *Féach na fáinleoga*!' (Swallows! See the swallows!) broke in on his reverie. Looking in the direction from which the whisper came, he saw a boy with close-cropped black hair leaning over towards a fair-haired girl. His heart skipped a beat: it was Jakki's son! Her head was visible just beyond the boy's left shoulder. On looking up he saw the reason for the whisper: high overhead, unseen by most of the congregation, two swallows were flying back and forth! How on earth had they got in? Another one of those unhappy accidents that life was constantly throwing up – like the time they had learned that Joanne had cancer. She had visited their GP for a slight chest pain and he had suggested she get an x-ray. It had all seemed so routine, a mere precaution – and then the dreaded word, the big C . . .

Since her death he had gone out with a succession of glamorous women but somehow he could never find the right combination of beauty and personality. Maybe it was out of respect for Joanne's memory that he couldn't bring himself to choose her replacement. It was she who had groomed him, a rough, self-made businessman, to be a senator – and yet in one important area he had resisted her wishes. She had begged him during those last days in the Mater to acknowledge Jakki's son but he had dug in his heels – nothing would ever induce him to accept that . . . that— His head was beginning to ache. Then he noticed the fair-haired girl looking at the boy the way Joanne used to look at him, and his wife's low, tired voice was whispering 'Tadhg, no matter what, he's your grandson.'

Unless he was listening intently, Aidan couldn't follow the priest's accent, so he allowed his mind to wander. If it weren't for Margaret he would probably skip church, but she liked going and he enjoyed being seen with her. He guessed also that Margaret realised his mother approved of young people having convictions and this influenced her decision to join them. Women!

Before long he noticed the swallows. Immediately he sensed that they were frightened. They must have flown in through a small window opening that slanted upwards but couldn't escape through the same opening. Now they were trapped above this great crowd of humans, who were totally unaware of their predicament. That was typical of people, so engrossed in their own affairs that they couldn't see how their actions affected other creatures. These swallows had come up from Africa, where even now his father was probably in some sort of danger. Back and forth they flew, from glowing window to glowing window, from dark rafter to dark rafter, until, tired and confused, they landed on a cornice, twittering plaintively. What could he do? Impulsively he leaned over to Margaret and drew her attention to the tiny visitors. On hearing his voice, Jakki frowned at him to be quiet.

Bent low like guerrilla fighters Johnno and Clint, each carrying a can of petrol, were sneaking through the trees opposite the weir. An hour earlier they had seen Jakki and Aidan leaving Cherryfield to walk towards the village, so they concluded that the lodge was empty.

Johnno was in a foul mood. On Friday, after a heated argument about his drug dealing, Tubby had thrown him out and he was again sleeping on the barge.

The previous evening he and Clint had siphoned petrol out of a truck parked at Euromart, filling the cans that had been used to burn his shelter. After a night of drinking, taking ecstasy and listening to rap, they were psyched up to act.

Donning balaclavas, they approached the lodge. There was no sign of life. To their delight, they found the door unlocked. Slipping inside, they hurriedly doused the sitting room furniture and the kitchen with petrol. They were about to enter the corridor adjoining the bedroom when a succession of deep honks followed by a dull bang shattered the stillness. Paul O'Neill or Ray Kelly must be trying to shoot the raven. It was dangerous to delay. Grabbing the bark mask, Johnno retreated, preceded by Clint, who had taken the ebony statue of the mother and child. There was another shot, louder this time, so the gunman must be drawing near.

Once outside, Johnno hurriedly spilled the last of the petrol around the entrance then tossed a lighted match into the kitchen. A wall of flame leapt out at them, singeing their sweaters and balaclavas. Dropping their booty Johnno and Clint took to their heels.

Chapter 23

In a pew near the back of the church Tubby tried to concentrate on the mass, but though he found the priest's African accent pleasant, it was difficult to understand. Mick Neary's reading of biblical extracts was more to his liking – that image of the new Jerusalem descending from heaven was really terrific; nevertheless, his mind was soon wandering.

For days now the words of the seventeenth century outlaw Sean O'Dwyer had been haunting him:

' '*S é mo ró-chreach maidne*
Ná fuair mé bás gan pheacadh
Sula bhfuair mé scannail
Fé mo chuid féin …'
('It's my great morning loss
That I didn't die sinless
Before I got disgrace
For my portion …')

Like O'Dwyer he loved the woods and wild nature, yet he too had lost out in life. His wife and children were gone: Matthew in Canada, Vivienne in Australia – or was it Thailand? His teaching career was an exercise in futility and his efforts to help Johnno had left a bitter taste in his mouth. Instead of accepting his offer to get him work as a waiter in the Castle Hotel, Johnno had ranted on about how badly everyone was treating him and how he would like to cut the throat of every friggin' adult in Lisheen. He would accept no responsibility for Darren Byrne's death even though he had supplied the ecstasy on which Darren had overdosed. Ah well, what could one expect with the world turning topsy-turvy? Short of dying, there was only one escape route: get out! As Sean O'Dwyer had said:

'*Anois tá an choill dá gearradh;*
Triallfaimid thar caladh . . .'
('Now the wood is being cut;
We'll journey overseas . . .')

There were millions of young people in Africa crying out for an education. He would ask Jakki to contact Give about a teaching job in Nirambia – even if the region had once been known as 'the White man's grave'. What was the use of remaining in a country that trampled on the riches, physical and cultural, which had been handed on by past generations?

In the midst of these gloomy reflections, his eye caught the flicker of wings and looking up, he was surprised to see two swallows flying high above the altar. Had they passed through Nirambia on their journey back from

South Africa? They must be an omen: here he was thinking about working for Give and these birds had appeared. Wasn't it the Romans who had used the flight of birds to decide whether or not an occasion was going to be auspicious? Yes, this was clearly going to be an auspicious day.

Ignoring Aidan's restlessness, Jakki tried to listen to the homily. The priest was telling a story about another priest, a friend of his, who was attending a dying man. The man asked to be laid out with a spoon in his mouth. Naturally the priest was surprised and asked the reason for such a request. The dying man said that when he was a child finishing his dinner his mother used always tell him to hold onto his spoon because there was something better on the way.

Jakki could recall a fairly similar scene: they were in a mud brick house miles from Lapano, the family sitting on a mat round a tray of steaming rice and vegetables, eating with their fingers, she and Maurice using spoons, and then at the end there was the shared dish of fresh pineapple segments. It was while John Morgan was driving them to such a meal that they had first encountered the rebels.

The Renault had conked out on a stretch of flooded road and she and Maurice had got out to push it. She would never forget the stifling heat and the mosquitoes and the stench of the stagnant water, which reached to above their knees. Suddenly half a dozen teenagers armed with Kalashnikovs emerged from the surrounding bush. They had expected to be taken prisoner or at the very least robbed but when Jakki managed to convey to them in her mixture of dialect phrases and English that she was Gbenga's woman the situation had been transformed. Obviously the name of Aidan's father commanded high respect, though these fellows had never met him and didn't know whether he was in the country or not. The rebel leader had ordered his band to shove their car through the flood. After that she had met them on a number of occasions, listening to their grievances and expressing approval for their campaign.

Oh, why couldn't she have minded her own business? What right had she, a foreigner, to criticise the government, even if it was corrupt? Maurice had paid dearly for her meddling. She had decided back then that government agents had carried out the murder, though they had made it look like a rebel attack. Probably she was the intended victim – but what if the rebels out of misguided loyalty to the absent Gbenga had decided to eliminate his woman's new partner? That was the ghastly possibility which, surfacing nightly from the depths of her mind, threatened her sanity. Poor Maurice . . . What had he done to deserve such an end?

'. . . a heavenly mansion, where we will be happy forever,' the priest's voice broke in on her consciousness.

He was delivering the traditional Christian message but with such conviction and simple faith that Jakki was touched. She could understand how people in Africa suffering from malnutrition, persecution and epidemics would be consoled by such a sermon. The only trouble was the competing versions of salvation: the Catholics in one part of Nirambia giving their set of guidelines, the evangelical Protestants in another part theirs and the Moslems in another part threatening to impose theirs – or at least their *Sharia* laws. Then there were the unconverted who held on to ancient tribal beliefs in spirits and fetishes. It was all part of our doomed attempt to penetrate the mystery of existence: why are we here? What lies beyond the grave? Maybe it was best to be like the dying man who asked for a spoon.

Aidan nudged her. '*Cad e?* (What is it?),' Jakki demanded. The silly boy was so much on edge over the plight of the swallows that he wanted to leave. Maybe she should go as well. The sooner she got back to the lodge the easier she would feel about Iyabo and Abosede. '*Beidh siad in ann eitilt amach an doras tar éis an Aifreann* (They'll be able to fly out the door after Mass),' she assured him as the three of them rose.

She, Aidan and Margaret made their way quickly along the side aisle, Jakki looking straight ahead to evade the barrage of curious glances. Once outside they paused to ask Margaret if she would like to walk home with them.

She had just agreed when a suave voice behind them made them turn around. It was Tadhg Higgins!

'Sorry for intruding.' He smiled at his daughter and Aidan as if uncertain of their reaction. 'May I offer you a lift to Cherryfield?'

Jakki's first reaction was to tell him what he could do with his lift then she looked at the two young people and changed her mind. Why should they be dragged into her quarrel?

'That's very kind of you.' She was icily polite.

'Not at all.' Mr Higgins beamed at Aidan and Margaret. 'You have a fine young man here, Miss Hannon.' He casually held out his hand and then, seeing that the gesture might not be reciprocated, just as casually dropped it. 'And I'll take it that you are his girlfriend?'

'No, we're just good friends,' Margaret replied, at which the senator grinned.

'That's not a bad thing to be,' he said. 'We all need friends. My car is just over there in the car park.'

Chapter 24

At first Aidan felt ill at ease, refusing to hold Margaret's hand until the engine purred into life. His mother sat in front of him in the passenger seat, gazing fixedly at everything as the Mercedes swung out into the road and cruised past the church and down into the village. One could have cut the atmosphere with a knife. Only Margaret seemed relaxed, exchanging chitchat with the senator about her interest in Irish and her holidays in the Gaeltacht.

'I've always held that we should make a better effort to revive our native language,' Mr Higgins said sententiously. 'It's the one thing that distinguishes us from our neighbours across the water. I only wish I could speak it properly myself.'

'Aidan is as good as any native speaker,' Margaret informed him proudly.

'So I've heard.' Mr Higgins glanced at his daughter. 'You've done a fantastic job in bringing him up.'

'I didn't have much choice.' Jakki didn't turn her face from the window as she spoke.

'Still, you're to be congratulated,' her father insisted. 'Your mother is a remarkable woman, Aidan.'

'Yes.' Aidan met his eyes steadily in the rear view mirror.

'You'll all have to visit me this afternoon,' Mr Higgins announced as if reaching a sudden decision. 'I'll speak to Mrs McShane about preparing some food.'

'We won't be going, Senator; not till you halt the destruction of the woods.' The words were out of Jakki's mouth before she could stop them.

'I've been mulling over that since your visit to me,' her father declared. 'There are certain things more important than financial rectitude. The half dozen chalets already contracted for will go ahead; the others will be cancelled. Of course, you'll have to get the remaining ecowarriors to leave. You don't seem overjoyed.'

'It's those six chalets,' Jakki was unyielding. 'They'll intrude on the habitat of the deer and wildlife.'

'Oh, come now,' there was a slight edge to her father's voice, 'you can't expect to get everything you want in this life. I'm going to erect wire fences around the chalets and golf course; apart from that, the deer will be free to roam through Cherryfield as they please. As a matter of fact, I had thought of giving you and Aidan one of the chalets while we renovate the lodge – we're practically family, you know.'

'No, I don't know,' Jakki snapped. 'Even six chalets will

disturb the wildlife.'

'*Stop, a Mham!*' Aidan broke in. '*Ná bí righin. Is fearr leath ná meath.*'

'I understand that!' Mr Higgins exclaimed. 'Your son is reminding you that half a loaf is better than no bread. And the young man is absolutely right.'

'And may I remind him of another proverb: *Is binn béal ina thost* (a silent mouth is musical),' Jakki retorted.

After that an embarrassed silence reigned in the car until they were alongside the demesne wall and Margaret noticed smoke rising from the area where the lodge was situated.

'Fire!' She pointed to the black plume expanding above the trees. Mr Higgins immediately stepped on the accelerator so that they reached the entrance gate in seconds. As Aidan got out to press the keypad the acrid smell of burning timber filled his nostrils. Quickly he jumped back into the car. When they screeched to a halt by the smoke-shrouded lodge they almost collided with Red, who was carrying buckets of water. To their right Ray Kelly and Paul O'Neill were using knapsack sprayers to douse the kitchen entrance.

'Have you sent for the fire brigade?' Senator Higgins shouted from the car.

'We have.' Ray wiped the grime off his sweating forehead with the back of his hand. 'They should have been here long ago. Red there spotted the smoke and raised the alarm.'

'Are the children all right?' Jakki felt a band of pain tightening on her forehead.

'I smashed the bars on the bathroom window,' Red avoided the question, 'but it was too hot to go in. Hey!' he yelled as Aidan darted past them in the direction of the kitchen. 'Come back! That roof is about to collapse!'

'*Fan liomsa* (Wait for me)!' Jakki ran after Aidan, followed by Red and her father.

'The bloody fools!' Ray fumed to Paul. He could hear the crunch of burnt timber as the four moved deeper into the interior, then Aidan's voice calling out, 'The tunnel!' What the hell could he be talking about? Whatever it was, he was doing no good waiting outside. Tying a wet handkerchief over his nose and mouth he entered the kitchen.

The heat and fumes from the smouldering debris were overpowering and the hot ashes burned his shins. Venturing on, he stepped over fallen tiles and blackened utensils into the cinder-filled shell of the sitting room. 'Where are you?' he yelled repeatedly as the voices of the others grew fainter.

An opening where a door had been led him into a narrow corridor half filled with smoke. Immediately he could hear muffled voices coming from what looked like the mouth of a tunnel. Stooping, he descended stone steps that led to a dark passage. The voices were closer now so that he pressed on, feeling his way with his hands. Eventually he could see blurred shapes moving against a wavering light. In a few moments he had reached the spot, a sort of crude chamber with brick walls that was relatively free of smoke.

The sight that met his eyes was like something out of a horror film. Red was holding a cigarette lighter, while Aidan and Senator Higgins bent over the prostrate bodies of two girls, and Jakki crouched in a corner, whimpering.

'Are they alive?' Ray asked.

'This one could be,' Senator Higgins indicated Iyabo. 'Her sister doesn't seem to be breathing. You and Red take the older girl and Aidan and I will carry her sister. Jakki, you hold the lighter.'

'Leave me alone!' Jakki shouted. 'I don't trust you. For all I know it was you who arranged to have the fire set so that you could get rid of us.'

'Mam!' Aidan cried. 'You don't know what you're saying.'

'It's all right, Aidan,' Mr Higgins handed him the lighter. 'We're all a bit distraught. Ray and Red, hurry it up there!'

'That's right, *Daddy*,' Jakki mocked hysterically, 'sweep it all away with a few soothing words. Two young girls are dead and all you're really worried about is how it will look in the papers. That's why you're here isn't it, to show your concern? But where were you when I was trying to look after my baby on my own? I was starving and you were parading around in the seanad making fine speeches about the homeless. And where were you when I had to go to Nirambia? I was afraid that if I stayed here watching you play the elder statesman while denying the existence of your own grandson I might go out of my mind. And where were you when Maurice was hacked to death?'

'Aidan, make your mother understand that she must get out of here and I'll manage this child on my own – she's not heavy.' Ignoring his daughter's accusations, Senator Higgins carried the limp Abosede into the tunnel.

'Stay away from me!' Jakki screamed at Aidan in Irish. 'I'm not leaving here. Go on and help your grandfather – oh yes, the senator is your grandfather. Now leave me. Can't you see that I can't help you anymore? I just bring death to anybody I love. It's all over now. All over . . .'

'I'm not budging, Mam.' Aidan crouched down beside his sobbing mother.

When Senator Higgins eventually made his way, spluttering and choking, back into the open, he found Margaret and Sky Hawk tending to Iyabo, who was lying on the ground with her eyes open. The men hurried over to relieve him of his burden.

'Aren't Aidan and his mother coming?' Margaret asked anxiously. 'Aidan!' she shouted, rising and rushing into the building.

Telling the others to remain outside, Tadhg Higgins wet a handkerchief and followed her.

By this time the ambulance had arrived, its flashing blue lights adding to the unreality of the scene. Red and Ray laid Abosede carefully beside her sister and as soon as they saw the paramedics racing up made to return to the tunnel. But before they could enter the kitchen, there was a sickening groan and the lodge roof collapsed in a cloud of ashes and sparks.

Chapter 25

On the metal end section of the barge deck the fire of dried sticks on which Johnno and Clint had heated their dinner was collapsing in ashes. Nearby, empty tinfoil containers lay in an untidy heap. They had nicked the food from Euromart the previous evening. Now, their hunger satisfied, they were drinking cans of lager while they listened to Bob Marley on the CD player.

Johnno was feeling invincible. The Hunting Lodge operation had been a complete success. Only a short while previously they had heard the siren as a fire engine hurried into Cherryfield. Squire Higgins must be ruing the day he had ordered his henchmen to burn the shelter. Johnno had even decided not to abandon the barge – running away could be taken as a sign of guilt.

Suddenly Clint spotted Youssou striding purposefully along the towpath, a heavy stick in his hand. Working feverishly, Johnno tried to untie the mooring rope, then cut through it with his flick knife. Youssou was now just twenty metres away. Lifting the wooden plank, Johnno used it to push the barge further out before letting it drop into the water. Without hesitating, Youssou jumped, reached the deck edge with one foot and simultaneously grabbed the handrail with both hands, dropping his stick in the process. Before he could climb onto the deck, Johnno swiped viciously at his arm with the flick knife. Emitting a cry of pain, Youssou threw himself backwards, hitting the water with an enormous splash.

'Why did you do that?' Clint protested.

'Shut up!' Johnno advanced on him with the flick knife. 'You're not my bleedin' father.'

'Hey, take it easy!' Clint backed away, eyes filled with dread.

This reaction maddened Johnno. Brandishing the flick knife, he rushed at Clint, who vaulted the handrail and fell, arms and legs out-thrown, into the canal.

'Help!' Clint bawled, splashing wildly. 'I can't swim.'

'Just a minute!' Youssou, who was standing dripping on the bank holding his arm, tore off his shoes and jacket and dived back into the water. By this time Clint had gone under, his head barely visible beneath a stream of bubbles. As soon as Youssou reached the barge Clint, thrashing his way to the surface, grabbed him about the neck with a drowning man's desperation. Using both arms, Youssou thrust outward and broke his hold, then hit him on the chin with his fist. Clint went limp. Before he could sink, however, Youssou turned him round, levered him into a floating position then towed him by the collar towards the bank, blood from his wounded arm staining the water.

Johnno watched impassively as Youssou clung to a sally branch with one hand and kept Clint afloat with the other.

'Aren't you going to help?' Youssou demanded.

'Help yourself, Blackie!' Johnno snarled. 'Nobody ever helped me.'

'I feel sorry for you,' Youssou cried. 'Have you no consideration for anyone, not even your friend?'

By this time Clint had recovered sufficiently to grab hold of the branch, allowing Youssou to pull himself up onto the bank.

'You're a bloody psycho!' Clint spluttered, glaring at the grinning figure on the deck.

A Dublin-bound train thundering past drowned out Johnno's answer.

It was pitch black in the underground chamber where Aidan and Margaret, Jakki and her father huddled, the lighter having finally given out. Smoke from the fire had accumulated higher up but near the floor there was still clean air. They had abandoned the idea of making a hole in the clay roof for fear it would collapse and bury them alive. Their only recourse was to wait patiently till they were rescued.

Jakki was calmer now, though occasionally she flared up, angrily accusing her father of negligence and hypocrisy. Aidan with his arm protectively around Margaret sat against the wall, trying to come to terms with the fact that he was the senator's only grandson. It was like being told that you were a totally different person from the one you thought you were – and yet for that very reason it was exciting. He had ventured into the tunnel as the son of Jakki Hannon, a school secretary; if he emerged – no, when he emerged – it would be as Aidan Higgins. But why had his mother kept him ignorant of his true identity? Was it simply to spite her father? If she didn't seem so close to cracking up he would demand an explanation. As it was, he wouldn't allow himself to be drawn into her attack on the senator. The priority now was to keep from panicking so that they would all get out alive.

'Give me your mobile and I'll try to contact Ray,' he offered.

'Fine.' His grandfather handed him the phone. 'And, Aidan, be careful: there's more smoke in the tunnel. Keep as low as you can.'

In a few minutes Aidan returned. 'It's not working,' he said. 'The battery must be run down – either that or the stuff filling the tunnel mouth is blocking the sound.'

'Never mind.' His grandfather took the phone. 'The fire brigade must be here by now.'

'We're all going to die here, Daddy, and there's not a thing you'll be able to do about it,' Jakki mocked.

'Nobody's going to die, Jakki,' her father replied gently. 'Do you remember when you were a child and I used to make up bedtime stories to help you go to sleep? Well, here's another one. There was this wicked giant who had a beautiful daughter whom he loved very much. He decided that when she grew up she should marry nobody but a prince whom he would pick out. His daughter, however, fell in love with a young man from a faraway country so the giant got very angry. In a fit of rage, he banished the young couple from his thoughts and vowed that he himself would become a prince. So he purchased a magnificent castle with great parks and woods and a fine lake and a herd of deer. But still he wasn't happy. There was something missing from his life, something that he couldn't even name but he knew that if he possessed it, he would really feel like a prince. Then one day when he was out riding he spied a lovely young woman and a young man entering the hunting lodge beside the lake. At first he couldn't believe his eyes: the young woman looked almost exactly like his lost daughter – am I boring you?'

'No,' Jakki murmured sleepily. 'What did the giant do?'

'He instructed his servants to made enquiries and lo and behold it turned out that the young woman was really his daughter. The giant was overjoyed but being a stupid old man he couldn't admit, even to himself, that he had been cruel and hard hearted. So he watched from a distance, hoping his daughter would make the first move. When her son – his handsome young grandson – broke into the castle looking for food, he turned a blind eye and when his daughter wrote articles attacking him for cutting down trees he pretended not to notice. Things went on like this for a long time until one day the lodge caught fire and the giant and his daughter and grandson – and his grandson's charming girlfriend – were trapped inside. The strange thing was that instead of being terrified, the giant was happy. For the first time since his daughter had left and his wife had died he was with people who were dearer to him than his own life and that he hoped would forgive him for his pride and foolishness. Was he too late?'

'No, not really,' Aidan said.

Jakki didn't answer. Her head was resting on her father's shoulder and she had fallen asleep.

Before the smouldering lodge, Ray and Paul were using dung forks to clear away the broken tiles and pieces of charred timber that a fireman equipped with a breathing apparatus was shovelling out the toilet window. Beyond them two other firemen directed a jet of water from a hose over parts of the interior that still smouldered. Red, whose partner, Sky Hawk, had departed in the ambulance with the children, was standing near a patrol car with two gardaí, who were questioning him about the fire. Suddenly, the fireman inside the window opening shouted that the corridor leading to the tunnel was open. Ignoring the representatives of the law, Red dashed forward to join in the rescue.

First through the bathroom window was a bedraggled Margaret, followed by Jakki, who looked dazed, and a cinder-smudged Mr Higgins. Behind him Aidan, refusing Red's proffered help, climbed out blinking into the afternoon sunlight. Immediately a camera clicked as a photographer from the *Lisheen Leader* arrived on the scene.

'No more photographs!' Mr Higgins ordered. 'How are the girls?'

'The older girl will be fine,' Ray told him. 'Her sister is in a critical state – the paramedics wouldn't comment on her chances. They should have reached the Mater Hospital by now.'

'Keep me informed of developments,' Mr Higgins instructed, before conducting Jakki and Margaret towards an ambulance that had just driven up.

'I'm all right.' Jakki shook his hand off her arm.

'I'm sure you are,' her father soothed. 'Still, there's no harm in letting the paramedics take a look at the two of you – just in case you've inhaled a lot of smoke.'

'And what about you, father?' she demanded. 'Weren't

you at the same risk?'

'I'm a tough old geezer,' he joked. 'Now, Jakki, trust me on this.'

'I will then,' she conceded reluctantly.

Smiling his gratitude, her father left them with the paramedics and returned to Aidan, who, watched by Ray and Paul, was being interviewed by a reporter from the *Leader*.

'Where is that fellow with the camera?' Mr Higgins asked. 'Hey, you!' he shouted to the surprised photographer. 'Come over here. I want you to take a photo of my grandson and me. If it weren't for this young man's courage there would be a more tragic outcome to this drama.'

The looks of puzzlement produced by his reference to 'my grandson' delighted Mr Higgins. He put his arm around Aidan's shoulder, grinning broadly. When the photographs were taken, the reporter pressed him for more information.

'Come to the house this evening and I'll fill you in,' he promised. 'In the meantime my grandson will tell you all about our ordeal in the tunnel. Go ahead, Aidan.'

There it was again, the puzzlement! Feeling younger and more elated than he had in years, Mr Higgins strode over to Garda Noel Morrison and his colleague, Garda Sheila Gately, who were again questioning Red.

'Hello, officers,' Mr Higgins greeted them warmly.

'You're talking to another hero. If Red hadn't raised the alarm, we'd still be waiting for the ambulance and fire brigade. Red, did you see anyone or anything suspicious when you first arrived here?'

'Yes, I did.' Red led the way to a flowering wygelia bush, against which the African mask and statue rested, alongside an empty petrol can. 'I reckoned you'd want those for evidence.'

'Why didn't you show them to us?' Garda Morrison demanded.

'I would have if you hadn't hassled me,' Red explained. 'They were thrown on the ground outside the kitchen door.'

'Thanks, Red.' Mr Higgins gazed fascinated at the sinister mask. 'You've been a great help. I'll see you're rewarded for everything you've done today.'

'The best reward you could give me, Senator,' Red looked him straight in the eye, 'is not to cut down any more trees.'

'We'll discuss that later,' Mr Higgins assured him. 'You and I have more common ground between us than my critics care to admit. Still, if no tree was ever cut down we wouldn't have this,' he added, bending to pick up the statue.

'Don't, Senator!' Garda Gately cried. 'We'll have to dust that for fingerprints.'

The ebony face gazed tranquilly at them and at the

firemen emerging from the charred shell of the lodge. From the protecting wooden arms the child gazed too, steadily, unblinkingly.

Epilogue

'I don't want to argue with you but I do feel betrayed,' Mr Higgins told his daughter. He was meeting with her and Tom Keating in the Indian room to discuss an article they had published in *Gael Glas* lamenting the desecration of Cherryfield. 'I thought we had reached a consensus about the development of the demesne, then my secretary sends me this.' He held up the newspaper.

'And we feel betrayed,' Jakki retorted. 'It turns out that the six chalets have now become twenty-six.'

'That was my solicitor's blunder,' her father assured her. 'I repeated in good faith exactly what he told me. If you wish, I can show you his letter revising the number.'

'I'm sure you can.' Jakki scoffed.

'We're not blaming you,' Tubby pointed out. 'We're blaming government inaction. Cherryfield is part of our national heritage and it should have been purchased for the nation. If Alicia MacMorris saw what we—'

'I don't mean to interrupt you,' Mr Higgins broke in, 'but your own colleague, Mick Neary, accepts that what we're doing is reasonable.'

'He would,' Tubby snorted, 'but then he's moving into Lisheen Gatehouse! When I see what our politicians have allowed to happen in this country, I cannot help recalling Captain MacMorris in *Henry V*: "What ish my Nation? Ish a Villaine, and a Bastard, and a Knave, and a Rascal". We have sold our heritage, Senator, for a mess of pottage.'

'I'm afraid I can't quote Shakespeare like you,' Mr Higgins's urbane voice had an edge, 'but hurling accusations at people who have to live in the real world is hardly productive.'

'Here we go again, Dad,' Jakki burst out. 'Everything has to be reasonable and productive and progressive. Meanwhile, the Celtic Tiger is gobbling up the very things we should treasure. Look at the situation around Dublin. Fifty years ago there was forest and farming land in plenty; today you have urban sprawl relentlessly devouring our green belt. And, of course, we must have recreational outlets for these suburbanites, so we turn a beautiful, historic demesne into a golf course. I saw the same thing in Nirambia, the nation's forests and minerals sold to multinationals so that the government could erect grandiose buildings to impress foreigners. It's like the days of the British Raj in India, the ruling elite despoiling the country for their own enrichment.'

'Easy on,' her father protested. 'You forget that I have a personal interest in seeing that Cherryfield is not despoiled.'

'No, I'm not forgetting,' Jakki stormed on. 'But why do you think Aidan is coming to Africa with me? It's because this is no longer a place where he cares to live. All the wildlife has been disturbed: the peregrines and ravens have left their nesting sites, and I was right, the herons are no longer on the island – at least I didn't see any when we were coming in. I'm told that the deer have already been culled and it's only a matter of time till they're all shot. We can't have them trespassing on the golf greens and the chalet gardens, can we? You know, John Cox and Clint Campbell were arrested for setting fire to the lodge and causing the death of Abosede but they aren't the real vandals. You are, Dad. How do you feel about having the death of Cherryfield on your hands?'

'Hold it!' Her father waved an impatient hand. 'Before you throw accusations like that about, you might recall that when the MacMorrises created this demesne they had an army of poorly paid servants to run it. I have to make it economically viable in the twenty-first century. And as for the chalets, the legal position is that I must honour existing contracts. You see, Jakki, it's easy for you and Mr Keating to take the moral high ground but I have to deal with hard economic facts. I've tried to act honourably in this matter – that's why I invited you here today rather than sue your paper for libel.'

'It doesn't matter anyway,' Jakki said in a calm, almost regretful voice. 'Tom, Aidan and I are going to Nirambia next month. John Morgan has invited me out and I'm taking Aidan so that he can experience his African heritage at first hand – I owe that much to Gbenga's memory. As for your plans to make him your heir, if you really love him, father – and I believe you do – if you really want him back, you'll have to create a new Cherryfield where man and nature can coexist in harmony. It's as simple as that, Dad. Otherwise, you may never set eyes on him again, nor on me either.'

Aidan and Margaret, who was carrying a bunch of wildflowers, were standing by a fresh grave on the edge of Fennor Cemetery. Unlike nearby graves, it had no headstone, only a plain deal plank, rounded at the top, on which was painted in black letters, *Abosede Ogundele,* and the dates of her birth and death. A smaller wooden plank stood at the other end. Somebody had stuck a bunch of shop flowers surrounded by their green plastic wrapper in the clay but apart from this wilting tribute, the grave was bare. Behind it the ruins of a medieval church half hidden by ivy, blocked the view of Darren's grave, which was located near the entrance gate. Finches twittered in the ivy, swallows jinked and glided overhead, bees hummed in the flowering elder trees and butterflies flitted from dandelions to wild rose blooms.

'*Ó dàbò Abosede* (Goodbye, Abosede),' Aidan murmured as Margaret laid the flowers on the grave.

'I wonder if she and Darren are in the same heaven,' Margaret said.

'Who knows?' Aidan shrugged. 'Do you remember what that priest said: "Hold on to your spoon: the best is yet to come"?'

'How can that be?' Margaret looked at him with tears in her eyes.

'Don't!' Aidan put his arm about her waist and pressed her to him. 'I've told you I'm only going to Nirambia to get to know my father's country. It's something I have to do. When Mam and I are fixed up, you can come out to see us.'

'You're planning to stay then?'

'I've told you already that whatever happens, you and I will be together. Grandad wants me to stay here and Mam wants me to stay with her – but she also wants me to get my Leaving Cert, so that means— '

'Cherryfield!' Margaret finished for him.

Aidan smiled into her grey-green eyes. 'Between you and Cherryfield I'm afraid Africa doesn't stand a chance.'

Also from Patrick Devaney

The Stranger and the Pooka
0-947548-85-8

'Patrick Devaney writes beautifully about nature.'
Vincent Banville, *The Irish Times*

'I wasn't going to read this book . . . I'm very glad I did.'
Books Ireland

The Psychic Edge

1-84210-020-3

'An exciting read, with plenty of intrigue to keep the reader guessing right to the end.'

Books Ireland